The Last

Book One

Other books by R. A. Steffan

The Circle of Blood Series

Circle of Blood: Books 1-3
Circle of Blood: Books 4-6

The Last Vampire World

The Last Vampire: Books 1-3
The Last Vampire: Books 4-6
Vampire Bound: The Complete Series, Books 1-4
Forsaken Fae: The Complete Series, Books 1-3
The Sixth Demon (coming soon)

The Eburosi Chronicles

The Complete Horse Mistress Collection
The Complete Lion Mistress Collection
The Complete Dragon Mistress Collection
Master of Hounds

The Love and War Series

Antidote: Love and War, Book 1
Antigen: Love and War, Book 2
Antibody: Love and War, Book 3
Anthelion: Love and War, Book 4
Antagonist: Love and War, Book 5

The Last

Vampire

Book One

R. A. STEFFAN & JAELYNN WOOLF

Author's Note

This book contains graphic violence and explicit sexual content. It is intended for a mature audience.

Table of Contents

One

I was six years old when I learned that human beings weren't supposed to have red, gaping holes through their chests. That's not the sort of lesson that a person ever wants to repeat — and yet, here I was, staring down at the corpse stuffed into my garden shed like a discarded marionette.

I'd only wanted to mow my freaking lawn. It was supposed to rain later today, and the grass in the back yard already looked ragged and unkempt. So much of my life felt out of control — was it too much to ask for nicely manicured landscaping? Around the edges of my thoughts, I could feel panic swirling, threatening to drag me back to the long-ago autumn day when a little girl lost her innocence and her mother in the space between one heartbeat and the next.

My unease had begun to build the moment I noticed the broken padlock on the shed door. That sinking feeling in the stomach; the realization that someone has been poking around in your stuff and has probably stolen whatever looked most valuable. In this case, that meant my lawnmower. Aside from that and the weed whip, the shed mostly contained a collection of seldom-used gardening tools that had seen better days.

Bracing myself for the loss of a couple hundred dollars' worth of equipment, I'd opened the door and peered inside. The good news was that the lawnmower was still there. So were the weed whip and the plastic gas can.

The bad news was that my access to them was blocked by the collapsed body of a man with a gaping gunshot wound through his chest. He looked to be in his early thirties, with tousled black hair a bit longer than was fashionable, and a face like something from the artwork of Raphael or Michelangelo. If one of the old masters had sculpted a dark angel, it would have looked like this man—tragic and beautiful and dangerous.

He was wearing black jeans, combat boots, a white tailored shirt with a couple of buttons undone at the neck, and a black leather vest, open at the front. The shirt was ripped and soaked with blood, the stain covering the entire chest area. And the flesh beneath—

I swallowed hard.

I'd like to be able to say that I immediately sprung into action, checking his vital signs and running back to the house to grab my phone and call the police. The truth was that I stood there for a really long time, frozen, my thoughts flying away to PTSD-land like frightened, fluttering sparrows.

There was no one else in sight. Every house in this neighborhood had a privacy fence around the back yard, the blank, six-foot wooden walls giving the illusion of isolation. I could see no sign of how he got here. The gate to the yard was closed and latched. No horrific stains or bloody handprints splattered the wood.

Paralysis finally broken, I crouched down on shaky, creaking knees. I reached a trembling hand out, feeling sick, and pressed it under the dark-stubbled planes of the man's jaw like I'd seen people do on TV. His skin was cool in the balmy afternoon air. Far cooler than it should have been. I couldn't detect the telltale throb of a beating pulse, though I made myself feel around the side of his neck thoroughly.

For good measure, I held my hand a hairs-breadth above his nose and mouth for long seconds, checking his breathing. Nothing. The dark angel in my tool shed was long gone, his body cooling to the marble chill of the statue I'd mentally compared him to.

I felt faint. Frightened. Useless. It occurred to me all at once that I might be in danger. Had the killer brought him here to hide the body? Was a madman with a gun even now sneaking around my property, ready to silence any potential witnesses?

My heart, which had been tripping away in a shocked, thready beat, pounded into triple time. I staggered upright, backing away from the shed door, suddenly certain that a murderer was lurking on the far side of the ramshackle structure, just out of my line of sight. I shook my head, trying to clear it, the headache that had been plaguing me all day throbbing in time with my thundering pulse.

I needed to get my shit together. I was losing it, and I had to stop. Whoever had done this was probably long gone. This wasn't rocket science. When someone dumped a dead guy on your property, you secured the scene as best you could and called the cops. I could do those things. They weren't difficult.

So… secure the scene.

I closed the door on the grisly tableau inside. The little hinged latch was undamaged. The padlock that was supposed to secure it was broken, but when I threaded the shackle through the latch and twisted it closed, it wasn't very obvious that it hadn't locked properly.

I gave a final nervous look around the yard — still empty and quiet. Exercising the better part of valor, I didn't look behind the shed to see if a murderer was crouched there. Instead, I retreated to the sliding glass patio door and yanked it open, slipping inside before closing and locking it. Why the hell had I never listened to Dad when he'd told me to buy a length of board to jam in the door's track as an added security measure?

Dragging in deep, steadying breaths, I hurried to the kitchen and grabbed my phone off the counter. Twenty-six years old, and this was the first time I'd ever dialed emergency services, I realized.

"*Nine-one-one. What is your emergency?*" The voice on the other end of the phone call answered promptly. She sounded bored.

"Hello. There's… uh… there's a dead body in my back yard shed. I was going to mow the lawn and —"

"*Your name, please?*"

"Zorah Bright." I spelled it out, forestalling the inevitable question about the 'h.'

The woman rattled off my cell phone number from the caller ID and asked me to confirm that it was correct.

"That's right," I said.

"*Address?*" she asked, still sounding like she wished her shift would hurry up and finish.

"Three-eighteen Evian Street, St. Louis, six-three-one-one-eight."

"*Thank you. Do you need an ambulance?*"

I blinked. "Not… really. The guy's dead."

"*Did you check his vital signs?*"

"Yes," I said. "His skin's cold. No pulse. No breathing. Big hole through his chest."

My nausea rose, and grayness threatened the edges of my vision again.

"*Police and ambulance services are on their way to your location.*"

Still with the ambulance. I wondered if they got a lot of people calling in dead bodies that turned out not to be dead.

"Okay," I said, and hung up.

I felt shaky, but wired. If I tried to sit down, I knew I'd be crawling out of my skin in five minutes flat, so I paced instead. I wasn't sure how long I'd have to wait. The idea was that they were supposed to get to you in only a few minutes, but I'd caught an exposé piece on the local news not too long ago about how slow police response in the city could be. Sometimes it took them half an hour or more. The talking heads on television had argued back and forth about how much of the problem was down to poor management, and how much was due to insufficient budgetary allocations.

No matter the cause of the problem, the practical upshot was that it might be a while.

Maybe the wait would give any murderers hiding in my back yard enough time to sneak away, so the ultimate police confrontation could take place somewhere besides my house. Preferably, someplace far, far away from here.

I checked the time on my phone obsessively, still pacing despite my throbbing head and aching body. The seven-minute mark had just passed when I heard pounding noises. I froze, my feet abruptly glued to the worn hardwood floor. It wasn't the pounding of police officers at my front door. There'd been no sound of sirens, and the sound was coming from the back of the house, not the front.

Heart in throat, I crept toward the sliding patio door. This hadn't been the noise of a fist against glass. More like noise from a neighbor working on some kind of construction project. But… it had sounded closer than that. I sidled up to the wall next to the glass door, feeling vaguely ridiculous as I darted a peek into the yard.

Nothing.

The pounding came again, and I chanced a longer look, not so concerned now about trying to stay hidden.

Thump.

My eyes were drawn to the shed.

Thump, thump.

The shed door rattled against its hinges ominously.

Crash!

The latch and one of the hinges tore loose, the door half-falling open.

My jaw went slack. I stared like an idiot at the damaged shed, watching open-mouthed as a figure stepped past the twisted remains of the door. Red stained the front of his torn white shirt, drying to a darker shade of rust around the edges. He staggered a bit, catching himself on the doorframe with one hand as he looked around, clearly disoriented.

Unerringly… inevitably… his gaze settled on the glass door, peering directly at me through a too-long fringe of black hair. Even from this distance, I could see that his eyes were the same color as the ice in the center of a glacier—a blue so cold and brilliant that they seemed to be glowing from within.

I stood unmoving as he approached, those eyes pinning me like a cobra mesmerizing prey.

He'd been dead. I was sure of it. He had a freaking *hole* in his freaking *chest*, for Christ's sake. And *why wouldn't my feet move*? He stopped on the other side of the door, and we regarded each other through the flimsy barrier of glass. His eyes still glowed with that unnatural blue light.

"Open the door."

His voice was muffled, but not so much that I couldn't make out a panty-melting British accent. My hand crept toward the little lever that controlled the lock without conscious thought. I gasped and yanked it back just in time, appalled at myself. I would have staggered backward a step, but my feet were still rooted beneath me.

His brow furrowed as if I'd surprised him, two tiny lines marring the perfect planes of his face. "Right, then," he muttered, and lifted a hand to the door handle. A single, sharp jerk and the inadequate lock popped open, the sliding door jumping a bit on its track in the wake of the force he'd applied.

He stepped over the threshold, frowning down at me. His skin looked like alabaster, it was so pale.

Run, I thought furiously. *Why are you standing here, you idiot? Run!*

"Apologies for this, pet." His voice was low—maybe even a bit distracted. His hand, when it curled around my nape, was gentle. His skin still held that unnatural coolness. "I don't normally eat and run."

My skin prickled into gooseflesh as he gazed down at me from a six-inch advantage of height. I opened my mouth, but my voice had fled at the same time as control of my limbs, apparently. I couldn't look away from his glowing, pellucid eyes.

The fingers tracing the fine hair at the back of my neck caressed my skin like a lover's. "Don't fight me. Don't be afraid. I give you my word—you won't remember a thing about this once I'm gone."

I stared at him.

You won't remember a thing.

No. I refused. I might not have control of my body, but I would *not* relinquish my mind. I still couldn't speak to tell him so. What the hell was happening to me?

He slipped around my body like a shadow, keeping a careful inch of space between us. The only point of contact was his hand, the touch sparking heat down my nerve endings despite the cool temperature of his skin. His fingers entwined in the tight, dark spirals of my hair, using the grip to ease my head to the side. My scalp tingled in response to the gentle tug.

Lips closed on the column of my throat from behind. Teeth nipped, searching for the tenderest, most vulnerable skin. A small noise escaped the blockage of my vocal cords. It was the kind of noise shared by both lovers and trapped prey, and not one I could ever remember making before.

Twin points of sharp pain pierced the side of my throat, replaced by drugged heat even before my gasp could wrench free from my lungs. The gasp turned to a moan. I would have swayed, but a second hand steadied me in place. A deep, drawing sensation seemed to pull straight from my neck to a place low in my belly that was growing heavy with liquid warmth.

Stop, I tried to tell my body. *You shouldn't be enjoying this — what the hell is wrong with you?*

What's *wrong* with you? It was a question I'd heard far too often, and not one that had ever received a satisfactory answer. Right now, I was undeniably getting off on what could only be considered an assault, sliding into a state of blissful lightheadedness reminiscent of a post-orgasmic haze.

A complete stranger had latched his teeth onto my neck and was drinking my blood. I knew what the tableau we made must look like, and I knew how impossible it was for it to actually be what it appeared to be. I also didn't care.

I didn't care that vampires apparently existed. I didn't care that this guy could easily kill me. I didn't care that I was moaning shamelessly, letting a complete stranger take more and more of my weight as I succumbed to the swirling pleasure of relaxation and acceptance.

I still cared a tiny bit that I was supposed to forget about all of this once the stranger left.

Not happening, I reminded myself firmly.

Vertigo had already started to overcome me when I felt the points penetrating my neck slide free—an unpleasant sensation amongst all the languorous warmth. Lips and tongue soothed the raw wounds, the feeling growing distant as insistent dizziness took up more of my attention.

"Easy, now," said a low voice. Hands guided me down to a flat surface, though the new position did nothing to ease the spinning sensation. "I'm truly sorry for the intrusion. Just have yourself a nice little kip, and forget I was ever here."

I was vaguely aware of the brush of fingers pushing my wild curls back from my face.

"No," I rasped, even as the darkness of sleep—or perhaps unconsciousness—beckoned. I was distantly aware of the sound of the patio door sliding open and shut.

No. I won't forget.

Two

"Miss? *Miss*. Can you open your eyes for me?"

My eyes fluttered open to find two cops crouching over me—a man and a woman. *Huh*? I let my head flop first to one side, then the other, trying to orient myself. I was… lying on the floor, in what would be my dining room if I actually owned a dining table.

Why was I lying on the floor?

I'd been having some kind of crazy dream—

"Miss?" It was the female cop, an edge of worry coloring her tone.

"Yeah, I'm…" I began, only to trail off in search of the right word. *Okay* didn't really seem to cover it, somehow. "… awake," I finished lamely.

"Are you Zorah Bright?" the woman asked.

"Yes," I said.

"Do you remember what happened?" asked the male cop. "You called nine-one-one."

I blinked, puzzle pieces starting to reassemble inside my scrambled brain. Then I sat up abruptly, every muscle in my body protesting the movement. My head swam, and the female cop shot a hand out to steady my shoulder.

The man. In my shed. He hadn't been dead. He'd broken the door and—

My hand flew to the side of my neck. It was smooth. Unblemished. I rubbed at the skin, not understanding.

"Take it easy, Ms. Bright," said the male cop. "We knocked on the front door but there was no answer. So we did a visual inspection through the windows, and saw you collapsed in front of the patio door. It was unlocked."

Sirens approached from the road out front.

"That'll be the ambulance," said the woman. "Go get the EMTs in here for her."

"No!" I said quickly, my thoughts whirling. I couldn't afford an ambulance ride, much less an ER visit. And if I tried to tell anyone what happened, I'd be lucky not to end up in a straightjacket. Did they still use straightjackets these days?

I shook my head, intending to clear it. Instead, it felt like my brain had melted and was sloshing around inside my skull.

"No," I said more calmly. "I don't need the EMTs."

In fact, there was every chance that I *did* need the EMTs, but I couldn't go down that path right now.

"You collapsed," the female cop said gently.

I thought fast. "No, I… think I just fainted. It happens sometimes. Low blood pressure." I swallowed, my dry throat rasping. "I just need to, uh, sit quietly for a minute."

The male cop helped me stagger to my feet and deposited me on one of the bar stools by the stretch of kitchen counter I used as a table. "Do you remember what happened?" he asked.

I glanced between them, noting that the woman had pulled out a pen and notepad, ready to take a report. Again, visions of being carted off to a psych ward danced in my head. They even had an ambulance waiting right out front to transport me to crazytown.

A series of knocks pounded against the front door.

"I'll let them know what's going on," muttered the male cop, heading for the front of the house.

I turned to the woman and cleared my throat. "Right. So… like I told the nine-one-one operator, I went out to the shed to get my lawnmower, and when I got close I saw that the padlock had been broken."

"Was the shackle cut?" asked the woman, pausing in her note taking. "Like, with bolt cutters?"

I shook my head. "No. It had just been… wrenched open, I guess."

She raised an eyebrow and made another note, but didn't comment.

"The door was ajar, but only by a few inches," I continued. "I opened it, and that's when I saw the guy with the gunshot wound in his chest."

"Can you describe him?"

More memories shook loose. "Uh… he was a white guy. In his thirties, maybe? Dark hair. Wearing black jeans, a white shirt, and a black leather vest. His eyes were blue…"

She looked up again. "His eyes were open?"

I hesitated. They hadn't been. "No, they were closed. Maybe I saw them later. Or… maybe I just thought they were blue."

She suppressed a sigh. "Go on."

"He was obviously shot through the chest. There was a lot of blood. I felt for his pulse, and put my hand near his mouth and nose to check for breathing. I couldn't feel anything, so I closed the shed door and put the broken lock back on the latch to keep it shut. Then I ran inside and called the police."

She nodded, still writing. "And what happened next?"

This would be the tricky part, I knew. "I was waiting in the house for you guys to arrive—I think it had been about seven minutes. I heard pounding coming from the back yard. When I looked out through the patio door, I saw the door of the shed shaking on its hinges. It burst open, and… well… I guess I must have fainted."

Movement in the back yard caught my eye as I related the last part of my tale, startling me. The second cop was poking around the damaged shed, examining the door and peering into the musty interior. The woman finished writing and lowered the notebook. The edges of her mouth tugged down.

"I see," she said.

Her colleague finished whatever investigation he'd been doing and came back inside. His gaze raked over me briefly, but when he spoke, it was to his partner.

"There's traces of blood on the floor of the shed," he said. "Doesn't look like nearly enough to have killed someone. Whoever it was must not've been in too bad a shape. The workmanship on the shed is shoddy, but it would still have taken a fair bit of strength to tear out the door latch and one of the hinges from the inside."

The female cop nodded. "She says she thought he was dead, so she locked the shed door and came in here to make the call. She heard pounding, saw the door rattle, and fainted when it burst open."

Now both of the cops looked sour.

"Am I in trouble?" I asked carefully. "It wasn't a prank call. I honestly thought he was dead."

The female cop sighed. "Here's the thing, Miss Bright. Your supposed gunshot victim might have grounds to press charges against you for felonious restraint. You locked him in a shed, after all."

"What?" My stomach twisted. "But… he was on my property! Don't I have grounds for… I don't know… trespassing or breaking and entering, or something? And—I told you—I thought he was dead! I was trying to protect a crime scene!"

The woman made a quelling gesture with one hand. "Try to stay calm, Miss Bright. The guy's not here anymore." She looked at her partner questioningly.

He shrugged. "There are no obvious clues to show which direction he took off in."

"Okay," said the female cop. "So the victim is gone, and aside from putting out a notice to local hospitals about any patients presenting with gunshot wounds, we don't really have a good way to find him, or even identify him."

"Assuming it even was a gunshot wound at all," the other cop muttered.

"Basically, unless you want to file an official complaint against him, we're willing to let this incident slide. You were trying to do the right thing, but you made a mistake. We can just call it an unfortunate lapse of judgment on both sides and move on." The female cop looked at me hopefully. It was pretty obvious that neither she nor her partner wanted the headache of trying to deal with this little mystery.

"All right," I said meekly. At this point, all I wanted was for them to be gone, so I could lick my wounds in private. My fingertips strayed once more to the unblemished side of my neck.

After a few more perfunctory questions about my contact information, they left.

"Oh, by the way," said the male cop. "The lock on your patio door appears to be broken. You should get that fixed. It's a security risk."

Gee, you think so? I couldn't help the sarcastic mental quip.

"I'll put it on the list, along with my broken shed door," I muttered.

He gave me another frown—the kind that said he didn't appreciate having to deal with sarcastic twenty-somethings who locked wounded intruders in sheds and then fainted while waiting for the police. If I were being brutally honest, I couldn't really blame him for that. I kept my mouth shut, and closed the front door behind them.

Once I'd confirmed that the squad car had gone, disappearing around the corner onto the main road, I sighed and let the curtain fall back. The stairs up to the loft I used as a bedroom loomed like a towering mountain. I stared at them for a moment, feeling every shaky muscle and every aching joint. Then I headed for the first-floor bathroom instead.

The cheap fluorescent lighting hurt my eyes as it illuminated the paleness beneath the light brown of my skin tone. I looked gray and pasty, dark circles under my sunken chocolate gaze. My kinky hair was half-flattened where I'd lain on it, the rest of it sticking out in every direction. God, I looked like a complete wreck. But I was a complete wreck without a visible mark anywhere on my neck. I leaned forward over the sink to look more closely.

Still nothing.

Was I going insane? Hallucinating? Should I have let the ambulance take me to the hospital for a psych evaluation? I rubbed at the tender skin of my throat, feeling phantom lips there.

I didn't imagine it, damn it.

But… now what? Vampires were real. Maybe. What was I supposed to do with that?

Falling back on practicalities, I splashed water on my face with shaking hands, and pulled my wayward hair into a ponytail. The pull against my scalp momentarily eased the throbbing of my headache, but I knew in an hour or two it would probably make it worse again.

I wandered listlessly to the kitchen, remembering that they always told you to eat and drink something after you made a blood donation.

Blood donation. I nearly laughed, but if I started I wasn't sure I'd be able to stop.

If memory served, orange juice and a cookie was the preferred menu at the Red Cross. I had OJ—no preservatives added, not from concentrate—but cookies were a no-go with all the gluten and sugar. I grabbed a banana instead.

I've been kind of a health disaster since I was a kid, and even more so since puberty. One of the few things that seemed to make any real difference was sticking to an autoimmune diet. The one that seemed to work best was a sort of extra-strict version of Paleo. That—along with regular yoga— made the difference between being a more-or-less functional member of society and being too sick to work half the time.

I drank my juice and ate my banana, debating next steps.

I knew what I wanted to do, and I also knew that doing it would be a bad idea. I wanted to call my father, even though I was fully aware that the conversation was likely to end in tears— metaphorically, if seldom literally these days. In many ways, Dad was all I had left since my mom died, so long ago. In other ways, I'd lost him just as surely as I'd lost her.

Right now, I wanted to hear my father's voice—even though the realist in me knew it was unlikely that our relationship would spontaneously repair itself now, some twenty years after the fact.

Twenty years.

Christ.

I felt a jolt upon realizing that we were only two weeks out from July Fourth — the anniversary of the day that a lone gunman shot my mother through the heart while she was giving a Senate campaign speech. I found myself reaching for my phone before I even realized I'd done it. If I was reacting like this, how much worse must my father be feeling about the upcoming reminder of our loss? I'd been so young when it happened that my memories of Sasha Hawkins-Bright were hazy. But Dad had been married to her for years.

The call picked up on the fourth ring.

"Hello?"

I took a deep breath. "Dad? It's Zorah."

A pause.

"Hi, Zorah. Why are you calling?"

Not *'How are you doing?'* Not *'Good to hear from you.'*

"I… uh… I was wondering if you knew anyone here in St. Louis that I could borrow some tools from?"

I'd grown up here. In this very house, in fact. The moment I'd hit eighteen, though, my dad had taken off like a shot. He'd moved to Chicago, and I hadn't needed to be a genius to understand that I wasn't invited. The one charitable thing he'd done for me since then was to let me take over the mortgage payments on the old family home. The house had been refinanced to take advantage of the large amount of equity he and Mom had paid into it, and the low monthly payments that were left were the only reason I was able to live in a decent single-family residence rather than a dodgy apartment somewhere.

"What kind of tools do you need?" came the flat voice from hundreds of miles away.

I dragged my thoughts back to the conversation. "A power drill and a circular saw. Or a Sawzall in a pinch."

"What do you need them for?"

My jaw worked, recognizing the moment when our conversation would start to deteriorate.

"Someone broke into the garden shed," I said, trying not to make a big deal of it when all I really wanted to do was pour the story out to him and have him tell me not to worry and that everything would be all right. *As if.* "The latch is broken and the door's half off its hinges. Oh, and I need to replace the lock on the patio door, too."

"All you need for the lock is a screwdriver and a strong wrist," he muttered over the crackling cellular connection.

"Yeah? Well, a screwdriver's not going to cut it for the shed," I said. "Trust me. I have to replace part of the door frame."

"You should already own those tools. That's just part of being a responsible homeowner."

My teeth ground together harder, and I consciously relaxed my jaw. "I should, but I don't. I can't afford them. Now, do you know anybody I could borrow them from, or not?"

"You know damn well I don't keep in touch with anyone from… back then." He paused. *"Just… go rent*

them from somewhere. I don't know why you need me to tell you that."

"Sure," I said tightly. "Okay. I'll just go rent them."

I thought he might mutter some half-assed goodbye and hang up then, but of course he had to get in a final word. A final reminder of my short-comings in his eyes.

"You need to be more careful about security. I mean... people coming onto your property like that? Breaking locks and getting into things?" He huffed, and I didn't need to see his frown or rueful head-shake in order to picture it, clear as day. *"You're going to come to a bad end one day, Zorah – just like your mother."*

"Uh-huh. Thanks for all your help, Dad," I said around the tightness in my throat, and disconnected the call.

Three

I stayed in bed for as long as I could get away with the following morning, hoping that the double dose of over-the-counter painkillers I'd taken would be enough to get me through the day. Unfortunately, while they might've taken the edge off a bit, it was pretty clear that the score was still Kitchen Floor — one; Zorah — zero.

I should've let them drag me to the ER yesterday so I could have gotten some decent pain meds. I should call into work and tell them what happened… except for the vampire part, obviously. My supervisor would probably let me take the night off, under the circumstances.

I didn't, though. There were bills to pay. Power tools to rent. Lumber and hardware supplies to purchase.

Adulting, man. The struggle was real.

Instead, I stumbled down the stairs that seemed to get steeper every day, and took a very long, very hot shower. I aimed the cheap plastic detachable showerhead at the tight muscles of my neck and shoulders, the pulse of water on the massage setting going some way, in combination with all the ibuprofen I'd downed, toward making me feel human again.

What I needed, I decided, was a hot guy to rub my back with oil before and after every waitressing shift. Well, my back, along with several other areas that needed more attention than they were getting these days. I felt the familiar pull of frustrated sexual need, and eyed the pulsing showerhead speculatively for a moment.

But, no.

Irritated with myself, I put it back in the bracket and finished my routine — lather, shave, rinse. People with chronic health problems weren't supposed to also be sex addicts. But I wasn't a damned freak, no matter what my string of exes had to say on the matter.

Jesus, Zorah — what the hell is wrong with you?

You're draining me dry, woman. It's not natural.

No one wants to date a goddamned nympho, Zorah.

Either popular culture had lied to me, or I was a magnet for the only men on the planet who didn't like horny women. So, yeah, maybe I was in the midst of a pretty long dry spell at the moment, but that didn't mean I was doomed to marry my seven-in-one massaging showerhead *quite* yet. Especially on a day when I was already running late for my shift.

I worked cacao and shea butter conditioner into my hair, and then rubbed moisturizer over my body. At least I'd gotten a polite vampire yesterday, and he didn't let me drop like a ton of bricks when he was done using my neck as a sippy cup. There wasn't a bruise on me unless you counted the dark smudges of exhaustion under my eyes.

Hair, makeup, clothing. I stood before the bathroom mirror, giving myself a calculated once-over. Passable, I decided, though the tips tonight might be a bit on the thin side. Normally, I seemed to possess a talent for motivating the male customers, at least, to tip well. AJ's City Broiler was a fairly upscale restaurant. The pay was shit, but with tips it was enough for me to stay afloat while still devoting time to my passion project, volunteering for the Missouri Mental Health Alliance.

At least my job allowed me to stay afloat as long as everything didn't decide to break at once. I brought my push mower and the weed whip into the dining room to discourage anyone from taking advantage of the broken shed door while I was gone. I looked around, my eyes lighting on a straight-backed wooden chair. I jammed the chair sideways into the track of the patio door, spanning its width so that the door would catch against the wooden legs if someone tried to open it. That still left a gap of a couple of inches, but it wasn't big enough for anyone to squeeze through.

House secured — for a given definition of secure, at least — I shoved my waitressing uniform in my backpack and headed for the bus stop. I did own a car, but apparently 168,000 miles was the limit of what a '96 Honda Civic's transmission could handle without making awful grinding noises and smelling like smoke whenever it was in second gear.

Who knew?

So, anyway, the Civic was in the shop while I tried to decide whether it made more sense to spend twenty-five hundred bucks on a new transmission or twenty-five hundred bucks on a different car. Since I didn't have twenty-five hundred bucks for either of those things, I wasn't in a huge hurry to make that particular call.

The bus ride was an extra forty minutes I could really have done without today, mostly because it was forty minutes where I had nothing to do but think. I'd done a fair job of avoiding just such a situation in the hours since what I had mentally labeled *The Incident*.

I felt like my reaction so far to The Incident was not exactly the paragon of mental health. Not that anyone had accused me recently of being a paragon of mental health. Or any other kind of health, for that matter. But feeling relieved by the revelation that vampires existed seemed… kind of strange? After all, it wasn't like I was happy about the idea of my jugular being on tap.

Really? said a little subversive voice in my head. *You seemed pretty into it at the time.*

Shut up, I told the voice.

It wasn't that I was happy about the assault. It was… the validation, I guess. All my life, I'd had this nebulous feeling, like there was something dangerous hidden beneath the fabric of the world. Something more than what you could see on the surface.

Some reason for my mother's senseless death, besides the delusions of a madman with a gun raving about people being possessed by demons.

In my darker moments, I found myself flirting with conspiracy theories in an attempt to force the world to make sense. Nothing too outrageous — no lizard people from outer space or little gray aliens abducting people for anal probes. Just… things that might explain why the world seemed so fucked up, and why the people who seemed most passionate about making things better so often ended up with their blood splattered across a stage.

I had absolutely no clue whatsoever how the existence of supernatural beings with a hunger for O-positive tied into humanity in general being a raging dumpster fire. I just knew that what I had seen yesterday proved beyond a doubt that there was more to the world than what we'd been told.

Or, y'know, it meant my mind had finally snapped in the wake of childhood trauma, and I'd become delusional. One of those things or the other.

The question was — what was I supposed to do next? So far, my response to this great revelation had been to sleep a whole lot, take a shower, and go to work. Somehow, I doubted Buffy would ap-prove. But, realistically, what else was I going to do right now? The bills still needed to be paid. I also had absolutely no way to track my neck-raping Hugh Grant knockoff, unless vampires were in the habit of visiting the ER to get their gaping gunshot wounds sewn up.

Given the guy's lack of a heartbeat, I was going with *no* on that one.

So here I was, pulling up to my stop with a headache, a vague sense of validation, and not much else to show for my brief walk on the paranormal wild side. I got off the bus and trudged to AJ's.

It was a slow afternoon.

My mind wandered as I stood at the drink station, staring at the practically empty seating area. I hated this shift—especially on Tuesdays. I usually angled for night shifts or lunch shifts since those were the busiest and had the best payoffs, but for whatever reason, I kept getting stuck with the crappy shifts like this one lately. The time in-between lunch and dinner when pretty much nobody came in.

There were only a handful of tables occupied, mostly booths along the back wall of the restaurant. The décor was not extravagant here, but it was pleasant enough. A bar and grill, AJ's was undeniably on the upscale side, but it wasn't a stuffy haute cuisine joint. It could get a little noisy here on the weekend nights. Never rowdy, but people still enjoyed themselves.

Brass hardware adorned posts painted a happy shade of Copenhagen blue. Gold and tan accents pointed the way to the well-stocked bar on the right side of the seating area. Mirrors gleamed behind hundreds of bottles, glassware, and the bartender making drinks for a couple of patrons seated along the barstools.

"Zorah, I seated two for you. Table twenty-six." The hostess said as I bussed one of my empty tables. Sure, we had bussers, but during the slow shifts they sometimes got sent home. And when they were gone, I cleaned my own tables, like today.

After emptying the dirty dishes into a plastic bin back in the kitchen, I washed my hands then returned to the floor and glanced at twenty-six to see what I had to work with.

One man was dressed in a suit and tie, while the other one, whose back was to me, looked more casual. Suits were generally decent tippers. I called them suits. In fact, I had been at this so long, I had a whole system in place for ranking customers in terms of their likely tipping levels. Call it profiling if you like, but without it, I'd probably never survive financially.

Of course, suits or no, making customers wait was not a good way to get tipped. I quickly grabbed the small tablet from my apron pocket, then checked my appearance and made my way over to the new table.

The pair sat across from each other. The one facing me as I approached was a handsome black man around the age of forty, dressed like a typical businessman — probably an insurance guy or a stockbroker, or something like that.

"Afternoon, gentlemen," I greeted them as I wrote the table number and scribbled some notes. "Can I get you started with some drinks?"

"We're ready to order, thanks," the suit answered. "I'll have a whiskey sour, and the lamb chops, medium, with steamed vegetables and a loaded potato." As I jotted the order, I couldn't help but get caught by his eyes. Though nothing unusual came through in his voice, those eyes were sad. Almost haunted.

"Very good," I said, finishing with my notepad before looking at the second man. "And for you?"

"Just a glass of Clos du Bois Merlot for me," he said in a familiar English accent.

I froze, my eyes widening.

My undead Hugh Grant looked up, meeting my gaze and lifting a swept brow. He looked a lot less... *dead*... than he had yesterday. In fact, he looked a hell of a lot better than I felt this afternoon. I wondered how much of that had to do with my unplanned blood donation.

"Problem?" he asked in a cool, urbane tone.

My eyes narrowed.

I wavered, considering my options, unsure whether I was willing to make a scene at a job I couldn't afford to lose. A million questions and accusations flew through my head while fake Hugh Grant just sat there, looking at me calmly as several different expressions flitted across my face.

For the most part, I was pretty good at figuring out what people wanted, and how to please them. That tended to happen when you'd spent years learning to satisfy customers for a living, but this guy appeared unmoved and unreadable as I studied him.

"I didn't expect to see you here today," I managed at length. "You're certainly looking... better."

His dark eyes sharpened with interest.

"Ah," he said. "So you remember that after all, do you?"

My heartbeat jumped a tick or two, pounding a little harder in my chest. I could feel my face start to flush at his reaction. Not for the first time, I was grateful for my dusky complexion's ability to hide pink cheeks.

"It's not really the sort of thing you forget," I retorted.

Jesus Christ. I was playing one-upmanship games with a *vampire*. What the hell was I thinking?

Both men remained silent for a moment until the business guy looked over at his friend. "You two know each other, Rans?"

I filed the name away. The vampire formerly known as fake Hugh Grant studied me silently for a moment—taking in my face, my reaction. His serious expression disappeared then, replaced with a smile that was one part reckless and two parts dangerous.

"Not yet," he said, his accent caressing the words.

I was still burning holes through him with my eyes, and I had to admit that the Hugh Grant comparison really only worked when it came to the voice. My disjointed impression from yesterday had been accurate. He had darkly beautiful features—symmetrical and sharply cut. The effect was softened by the sweep of his very fine, very smooth black hair, which fell into the sort of messy waves that rock stars probably spent hours perfecting.

He didn't strike me as the type to spend hours in front of the mirror with his hair. He *did* strike me as the type to get himself shot through the chest and then gatecrash an innocent waitress's day off to drink her blood. But, of course, I might be a bit biased on the subject.

He tipped his head to one side, still regarding me with interest.

"Meet me after your shift is done," he said with casual confidence.

I frowned at him, my heart still pounding. "Why would I possibly agree to that?"

It wasn't that I was afraid of him, exactly, but that didn't mean I trusted the guy either. Still, something had changed in me yesterday. Some epic, glacial shift inside my soul.

Those ice-blue eyes saw right through me. "You'll agree because you're dying of curiosity," he said. "And because you weren't supposed to remember me."

Arrogant bastard. He was one hundred percent right, too. What I was about to agree to was crazy. I couldn't call the cops about him. I couldn't even drag some poor coworker along with me to act as backup, unless I wanted them to see me babbling about vampires and gunshot wounds. Yet I was going to do this anyway.

"Okay. I'll come," I said after a moment's hesitation. "I get off shift at six... but I have a couple of conditions."

Four

"Conditions?" the vampire echoed, watching me with well-hidden amusement. "Very well. Name them."

"I'll only meet you in a public place," I said, thinking fast.

"Of course," he replied easily. "There's a bar across the street. It should be well enough attended after six p.m."

I nodded. "All right. Make it six-thirty, though."

"Fair enough. And your additional conditions?"

I'd been mentally running through the list of people I knew decently well. It hadn't taken long. "I'll be arranging check-ins with a friend. If I don't contact her every ten minutes, she'll call the police with my description and have them come to the bar."

I wasn't entirely sure that the police would even agree to do something like that, but I made myself hold that glacier-deep gaze evenly, my chin tilted up, fake confidence oozing from every pore.

He probably didn't buy it any more than I did.

"Very sensible," he replied, without any overt indication that he was mocking me. "We have an agreement, then. You get my friend his lamb chops, and I'll meet you across the street at six-thirty, ready to hold a conversion in neat, ten-minute increments between phone calls."

All right, so he probably *was* mocking me. I could still be the bigger person here.

"Certainly," I said in my brisk waitress's tone. "I'll get this into the kitchen right away. Can I get you some bread while you wait?"

"That depends," he said. "Is there garlic butter?"

His companion gave a soft snort. "We're fine without bread, thank you," said the man in the suit, shooting Rans what I took to be a quelling glance.

The corners of Rans' eyes crinkled. "Yes, quite. Though that merlot can't come soon enough. I do so enjoy a nice, full-bodied red."

I shot him an unimpressed look and pivoted on my heel.

Despite the early hour, the restaurant started filling up. I delivered the merlot and the whiskey sour, and later, the lamb. My interactions with table twenty-six were the picture of professionalism, but those speculative blue eyes were seriously throwing me off of my mental game. Was the other guy a vampire, too? Did vampires request that their lamb chops be cooked to medium? Did they eat lamb chops and steamed vegetables in the first place?

The pair took their time, but didn't linger unnecessarily once the one-sided meal was finished. I presented them with the check and took the businessman's proffered credit card, making a mental note of the name—Guthrie Leonides—as I ran it. He signed the receipt when I returned to drop it off with his card, and I watched the two of them from the corner of my eye as they prepared to leave.

Rans pulled a green bill from his pocket and dropped it on the table, then the two of them headed for the door, not looking back. I glanced at the clock in the kitchen to see how much time I had before my six-thirty meeting.

It was three forty-five. A little less than three hours to go.

"I can do this," I whispered as I walked to their table to pick up the receipt and the tip.

A hundred dollar bill sat next to the empty wine glass.

My eyes grew wide at the tip lying crumpled on the table. The man who had broken into my house to drink my blood yesterday had just left me a hundred-dollar tip on a fifty-dollar meal. I blinked down at the wrinkled Benjamin. He might be a supernatural neck-rapist, I thought, but at least he wasn't a cheapskate on top of it. I picked up the bill and put it carefully away, along with the signed receipt.

"I can do this," I repeated, turning my attention toward cleaning off the table. I had about two and a half hours left to convince myself that I wasn't lying through my teeth.

Six p.m. came and went. I clocked out, changing clothes in the restroom and putting my uniform in my backpack to be washed before my shift tomorrow. The last couple of hours hadn't been enough time to convince myself that what I was about to do wasn't the dumbest idea I'd ever had. That wouldn't stop me from doing it, though.

Sometimes, you just had to live dangerously. I mean, how else was I going to find out what the hell was going on here? I'd been bemoaning my inability to track this guy down. Then he had quite literally *walked into my restaurant and sat down at one of my tables*. On the one hand, it seemed impossible that it could be a coincidence in a city of three hundred thousand people. On the other hand, I'd have to be nuts not to jump on the opportunity it presented.

I tossed my bag on the counter by one of the sinks while I scrolled my phone for a safety call. Although I didn't have a ton of close friends, I at least had a couple of people I could turn to in a pinch. Like Vonnie. She was one of the few people I spent any significant amount of time with whom I both liked and trusted. She was also a volunteer at MMHA, which was how I'd met her.

Honestly, we didn't have a whole lot in common beyond that. Vonnie was a single mom, and I was just… single. But we got along well enough. Enough for me to trust her with something like this.

"Hey, Zorah," Vonnie answered on the third ring, a bit of surprise coloring her tone. "What's up?"

"I need a favor," I said, trying one-handed to get my hair under some semblance of control.

"Sure," she said amiably.

"So, I met this guy…" My voice trailed off as I tried to figure out what I would actually say. Possibly I should have put a bit more forward planning into this call—not that Vonnie really needed to know the details of how I met Rans. "Anyway, he wants to meet at a bar on the Landing in a few minutes. But of course, I don't know him that well, so… can you be my safety call tonight?"

"Happy to," Vonnie said. She sounded overly cheery, probably excited at the idea that I had a date.

If only it were that simple, I thought. Hell, I could hardly remember the last time I had a date. Or even a one-night stand, for that matter.

Okay… that was a lie. I did remember, as much as I tried to forget.

It was two months ago, with Dan. Things were going well between us, actually. We'd been seeing each other for about a month. As per usual when I was pursuing a serious relationship, I'd refrained from sleeping with the guy until I thought things were solid between us. We had several things in common, and I was feeling confident that we had a future together.

Of course, it only took two sexcapades for things to turn south. He stopped meeting me at work. Stopped texting. Stopped calling. Didn't return *my* texts or calls. Finally, I got a single text telling me that he just didn't feel like we were compatible, and would I please not contact him anymore. The sad part was, it had been one of the more civil breakups I'd had over the past ten years.

At this point, I was starting to wonder if I was just really bad at the horizontal mambo, or if something was wrong with me mentally, or what. I always felt better when I had a sex partner. I was happier. I even felt physically healthier. And most of the time, I could find a guy to date easily enough when I put my mind to it. Hell, half the time I seemed to attract men even when I didn't want to.

But as soon as I slept with them?

Bam.

Dumped.

The universe was obviously trying to tell me something. But unless the message was 'LOL, you suck,' I just wasn't getting it so far. One of these days, though, it'd be nice to find someone who didn't run for the hills the moment after they shagged me.

"Zorah?" Vonnie's voice broke through my haze.

"Yeah, sorry. What were you saying?" I asked.

"I asked, who's the hunk?" Vonnie's smile could be heard right through the damned phone speaker.

Focus, girl. "Oh. Just a guy I met, um, at work."

"Awesome. If all goes well, I expect a full report, all right? Have pity on the single mother. I'm dying for juicy gossip."

"Deal," I said. "Here's hoping I won't need your rescue services this evening. I'll be at Studio 88 on the Landing. I'll check in every ten minutes, and let you know when I'm leaving the bar."

"Wow, you're not kidding around, are you?" Vonnie said, laughing. "I'm sure it will be fine.

Okay — you're running out of time. Go get him, tiger. If you miss a text, I'll text you and give you a minute to reply before I panic. Talk to you later."

I took a deep, steadying breath. "Thanks, Vonnie. You're the best."

We hung up. I slipped the phone in my pocket for easy access, and started a list in my head of all the things I wanted to ask this guy, repeating it to myself over and over so I wouldn't forget anything. After all, it could be the first, last, and only shot I had at my interview with a vampire.

Anne Rice, eat your heart out.

At twenty-five past six, I sent Vonnie a text letting her know I was about to meet my date, because telling her I was about to meet the man who broke into my house yesterday would have been too weird — even for me. She wished me well. I took a deep breath, threw my bag over my shoulder, and headed across the street.

Every nerve inside me was taut. My hands were shaking.

I stared at the glass doors leading into to Studio 88. Were the damned butterflies doing cartwheels in my stomach just due to nerves over what kind of answers I might be about to get to my questions… or was I walking into a trap I'd never come out of?

Maybe my imagination was running away with me again. If this guy had wanted to kill me or kidnap me, he could have done it yesterday at my house with nobody around. But he hadn't. He'd even reassured me that he wasn't going to hurt me—though I intended to have a word with him about how shitty I'd felt afterward.

If he was supposed to be a terrifying creature of the night, he wasn't a very good fit for the role. And why the hell did he leave me a hundred-dollar tip? Who does that?

I blew out a breath. Vampires, apparently. Next time, I'd make a point of offering him a second glass of Clos du Bois.

"Stop it," I admonished myself. I could do this. I'd said so a hundred times today, and that meant it had to be true. Right?

I inhaled slowly, taking in the mix of scents floating around the Landing. The Mississippi was behind me, a cobblestone street was beneath my feet, and a vampire lay before me, assuming he'd showed up as promised.

One step at a time. Shaking off my nerves, I reached for the glass door of the lounge and pulled it open. The second I crossed the threshold, I saw him. He sat alone at a small table in the back corner. Sipping a glass of red wine, just like earlier.

The lounge was dimly lit, giving it a cozy atmosphere. Candles in holders burned on several tables, and soft jazz emanated from speakers inset into the vaulted ceiling.

As though he'd somehow heard my restlessly circling thoughts, he turned his head and looked right at me. I stood tall under that cool blue gaze—or as tall as I could at five-foot-four, anyway. I kept my shoulders square and my chin up, refusing to show anything other than confidence.

Even if I didn't feel very confident, I sure as hell wasn't going to let him see it. With my lips turned down in a scowl and my head held high, I strode through the bar toward the dark, handsome stranger.

Rans stood as I approached, nodded a silent greeting, and pulled out a chair for me. That threw me off, but I was determined to keep my cool. I let him seat me, unused to being on the receiving end of that sort of effortless chivalry.

"You came," Rans said. "I'm glad."

I settled my backpack on the floor at my feet, not ready to give ground. "You should know that my friend is on standby, as promised. She's going to call the cops if I don't check in every ten minutes."

Rans let out a faint huff of what might have been amusement.

"I consider myself warned," he said, tilting his head as he studied me. "Now, can I get you a drink?"

"Sure. Something sweet, with a kick." I had a feeling I was going to need it.

He nodded. "Sweet and with a kick it is."

I kept my gaze on him as he walked up to the bar, ordered me a drink, then came back and set down a glass of something green on the rocks before seating himself across from me.

I sipped the melon-flavored liqueur, hoping some liquid courage would push me along. The Midori sour was, indeed, very sweet. And it definitely had a kick. I hadn't had a drink in weeks, and I hadn't eaten much since breakfast, so the alcohol went straight to the filter between my brain and my mouth.

Inhaling, I squared my shoulders and pushed back the half-finished drink.

"So, you're a vampire." Though it was meant to be a question, it came out more as a statement.

"And you're an enigma," Rans retorted, not bothering to deny the allegation. "Nice to meet you properly."

"You drank my blood yesterday," I said, keeping my voice level, like his penchant for guzzling other people's hemoglobin was no big deal.

"Yes." His answer was as simple as my question.

"But there's no wound on my neck," I pointed out — quite reasonably, I thought.

"No, there wouldn't be," he said. "My blood and saliva have strong healing properties. Your throat healed in moments."

I swallowed hard. "Am I going to turn into a vampire now?"

He laughed — a single bark, with a noticeably jagged edge to it. "No, luv. Not hardly."

"But now you're stalking me," I accused.

He shrugged. "A bit, yes. I did mention you're an enigma."

"What does that even mean?" I asked in bewilderment. "What about me is remotely enigmatic? I'm a broke-ass waitress working at a bar and grill."

"Your blood," he said, his eyes studying me carefully. "It's unusually... what's the word I'm looking for? Stimulating."

I shivered a bit, unable to stop myself. Then I promptly changed the subject.

"Who shot you yesterday?" I asked.

Rans looked amused at that. "A man with a shotgun."

My frown appeared to have no effect on him. "Why did he shoot you?"

"Someone told him to, I expect."

"So someone's trying to kill you?" I pressed.

"Kill me?" He snorted. "With a gun? No, that was more of a love-tap, really." His expression sobered. "Or a message, I suppose you could say."

I blinked at him. "What kind of a message requires a shotgun blast through the chest?"

He shook his head, impatient. "It's not important. What's more important is what you're doing walking around in broad daylight with blood like that running through your veins."

I paused to try and parse that statement, without success. "I have absolutely no clue what you're talking about," I told him truthfully.

"Really? None at all?" His gaze sharpened again, and it felt like he could see straight through my skull to what lay beneath. I didn't like the feeling. When he spoke again, his tone was thoughtful. "You actually mean that, don't you?"

I threw my hands up, frustration overflowing. "No, I'm lying to you. Vampires tear my shed door off its hinges and drink my neck like a Capri-Sun on a near daily basis. I thought that was a normal part of life. So, do you maybe want to... I don't know... explain some of this?"

He seemed to consider my words as he studied me closely. For a moment, he looked like he wanted to eat me alive—and not necessarily in the bad way. A frisson raced up my spine, but before I could decide whether to run for the hills or call him out on it, his expression smoothed into something like regret.

"Best not," he said, not unkindly. "You were supposed to forget what happened yesterday. If you're smart, you'll try your best to do exactly that. Go home, and stop asking questions that might draw the wrong kind of attention."

I bristled. "Oh, yeah? Questions like, 'Who's going to pay for the repairs to my shed?'"

He laughed, then—a low, pleasant sound that did things to my overactive libido despite my best efforts to maintain my armor of outrage. With a crooked smile, he reached out, brushing my cheek with the backs of his knuckles—a fleeting caress that left my skin warm and tingling where he'd touched it.

"What did you think the hundred-dollar tip was for, Zorah Bright?" he asked.

And then he was gone. I sat frozen for a moment, my hand rising stupidly to cover the echo of his touch on my cheek. By the time I came back to myself and hurried after him with Vonnie's worried check-in text buzzing at my hip, he had already disappeared into the city.

Five

He knew my name. I lay awake, staring at the early-morning darkness above me and trying not to freak out. Okay, yes, I was a waitress. I'd been wearing a nametag when he and his friend had come in to AJ's. A nametag with my *first* name. Not my last.

I'd slept poorly. What a shock, right? But the practical upshot was, I still felt weak and achy and generally like shit, two days after being drained by a vampire. How much had he taken from me? Should I be worried?

I spent an unproductive hour of my quality time with insomnia, trying to mentally tweak my budget this month to accommodate a trip to my doctor. No way in hell. Now that I was no longer on my father's health plan, I was uninsured— bringing in too much money to qualify for assistance with the premiums, but not enough to make the cheapest qualifying plan work. At least, not if I also wanted to eat and pay the utilities.

It didn't matter. I couldn't exactly tell the doctor that I was suffering from blood loss when I didn't have a wound to explain it. He would just start harping on about chronic fatigue syndrome again. Still, it was worrying. I'd managed to reach a balance between what I was physically capable of doing in a day, and what was necessary for my job.

Sure, it required taking more pain medication than I would have liked, but I'd been getting by. Right now, though, I felt like I'd been run over by a bus… and I was due at MMHA bright and early this morning, followed by an eleven to three shift at AJ's.

I sincerely doubted that the neglected lawn was going to see any attention today.

Since sleep was clearly a distant dream at this point, I slipped out of bed, drank a bunch of water, and ran through a gentle yoga routine while I waited for the sun to rise. Every joint ached, every muscle burned with fatigue after hours of doing nothing more strenuous than lying awake in bed. As it always did, the yoga helped a little, and a hot shower helped a little more.

This morning, I succumbed to the lure of the massaging showerhead. I still felt like a damned nympho freak, but I craved the brief flush of endorphin-fed physical and mental relief that would follow. By the time I'd eaten a solid breakfast and popped a few more ibuprofen, the prospect of heading out and working until three no longer made me want to hide under the covers and burst into girly tears.

At eight-thirty sharp, I strolled out of the spitting rain and into the bustling offices of the Missouri Mental Health Alliance; ready to add my paltry support to a cause I cared about. Before a sharp downturn in my unpredictable health had derailed my college career, I'd managed most of a two-year degree in accounting. That was what I did at MMHA—keep the books.

The unfinished associate's degree had originally been intended as a stepping-stone toward becoming a CPA like my father. Looking back, it had been a young woman's attempt to make an emotionally distant father love her, and a fairly sad attempt, at that. I didn't have any particular interest in a career in accounting, and at this point in my life it would have been difficult to pursue it further in any case. But it did mean I could offer a valuable service to MMHA.

That, I *did* care about.

In the absence of any grand explanation for my mother's assassination when I was little, I was left with a very troubled man who'd done a very bad thing in a moment of madness, and who had subsequently hung himself with his bed sheets in prison. By supporting an organization seeking better mental health care and screening, I could feel like I was making a difference, however small. So I volunteered.

Today, though, I walked in to find the place in barely controlled chaos.

Daisy, my boss, was pacing up and down the tiled floors of the MMHA front office, brandishing a stack of documents. "What the hell are we going to do about this?" she snapped.

Papers from another stack on the front desk flew around the room when the wind from the front door I'd just opened caught them, sweeping them around the foyer.

"What's the matter?" I asked, watching Daisy cursing and rifling almost frantically through what papers were left on the front desk. Vonnie shot me a wide-eyed look as she scrambled around, trying to help me pick up the papers that were now scattered across the floor.

"I got an email this morning." Daisy put the papers aside and stood straight, hands on her hips as she glowered at me.

Daisy was one of the few paid employees at MMHA. She was in her mid-thirties. Tall. Thin. Skin darker than mine, with large brown eyes. She always looked lovely, with lips painted deep red and the cutest wigs.

Today, she was rocking a cropped wig. Classy, yet hip. Her lips were pursed, and she was clearly pissed off. Just as clearly, I was the subject of her ire.

I laid the papers I'd rescued on the desk I usually sat at and squared up to her, figuring it was best to take the bull by the horns. "Take a breath, Daisy. Tell me what's wrong, and what can I do to help."

She shook her head, visibly trying to rein herself in. "The damn state auditor's office just emailed me. They want to schedule a meeting to discuss some 501C(3) filing irregularities they found." Her deep brown eyes bored into me. "Papers *you* filed, Zorah."

I wondered if people ever grew out of that sinking, sick, childhood feeling of being called out by the teacher—singled out in class and told you'd done something wrong. Or maybe that was just me?

Taking a moment to breathe and tamp down any defensive or emotional reaction, I made myself consider her words objectively. Could I have made a mistake? I wasn't a CPA, just a woman with most of a two-year college degree. That said, I was pretty sharp at the whole thing. I didn't slip, not when it came to money—another reason I managed to survive in south city on a server's income.

Being good with finances was one of my precious few super powers.

"I'm sure it's just a misunderstanding," I said, neatening the pile of papers. "I'll take care of it."

"I'm holding you to that, Zorah." Daisy said seriously. "The auditor asshole will be here at nine o'clock tomorrow morning. This is a big deal."

I nodded, feeling fresh stress settle like a weight on my chest. "I don't work at AJ's tomorrow. I can be here. Daisy, I'll get this sorted out. Trust me."

Some of the tension in Daisy's shoulders melted, and she nodded.

"Good," she said, picking up another stack of papers. "Here. These invoices came in yesterday. They're due ASAP."

Her expression settled into something slightly less terrifying, and she patted me on the arm before she disappeared back into her office. I let my breath out. For the most part, Daisy was more bark than bite. She may have been one of the few paid employees here, but with a teenage daughter who'd attempted suicide twice in the past couple of years, this job wasn't just a job to her. It wasn't just a job for any of us.

We all had something invested in this venture. We all had something to gain by its success, and we all had something to lose by its failure. To be honest, this volunteer work was one of the few things that actually meant something to me.

Healthcare — including mental healthcare — had been one of my mother's most important political platforms when she ran for office.

From all accounts, Sasha Bright had been an exceptionally charismatic woman. I didn't remember very much from back then, but I remember her being beautiful. Loving. Dad said she was popular and successful growing up, and that's how she ended up in local and state politics before running for a vacant US Senate seat.

I'd really looked up to her. All she was. All she stood for. Maybe I'd been too young to grasp everything about what she was doing, but I knew she was making the world a better place, not just for me and Dad, but for others. That's really what pushed me to work for the non-profit. I wanted to work at something bigger than myself.

Even twenty years on, I thought of my mother a lot at this time of year, so close to when she was killed.

The older I got, the more passionately I promised myself two things. One, I'd find out what really happened to her, and two, I'd do something significant. Stand up for others who maybe couldn't stand up for themselves. It felt like the least I could do.

"Need any help?" Vonnie Morgan—my safety call from last night and one of the few people I'd actually call a friend—approached, holding out the papers she'd picked up from the floor.

"God, yes," I told her. "Can you help me get these invoices processed?" I gestured to the pile Daisy had handed me.

"Sure thing. I hate to say this, but you look like shit, honey," she said, her eyes narrowed. "Rough night?"

"You have no idea," I said with feeling.

Vonnie was the single mother of a teenage boy. He was about thirteen, I was pretty sure. She was also an amazingly strong woman, and I was a bit in awe of her. Hell, she had her kid when she was just a baby, herself. Sixteen. After dealing with a deadbeat dad who disappeared and never lifted a finger to support their kid, Vonnie still somehow managed to make ends meet and also volunteer her time.

I sometimes felt like I'd had it rough, but truth be told, I had no idea how she managed it all, supporting two people on a lowly retail salary. Vonnie was strong as steel. With only occasional babysitting help from her parents, she took care of business. Outside of MMHA, she worked two jobs and had recently started going to night school to be a paralegal.

In my eyes, she was a freaking rock star.

"So…?" Vonnie stared at me, drawing the word out and batting her long lashes as she waited for me to indulge her with some dirty details of last night.

If only I had dirty details... or anything I could share. Somehow, I doubted she wanted to hear about my quality time in the shower.

"C'mon," she wheedled, pushing long, red hair off her shoulders. "Spill."

She picked up papers from a chair beside my desk and sat, laid the rest of the papers in front of me then stared at me, unblinking. I gazed back blankly, still fresh out of words. It's not like I could say much about the frankly bizarre meeting.

I'd been silent too long.

"Oh, come on." She narrowed her gaze. "Something happened last night." She pointed at me, eyes insinuating I was holding back. "You only texted me once. Was it horrible? Did he have radioactive bad breath? Give me a little something to work with, here!"

I rolled my eyes. "No, he didn't have radioactive bad breath."

"Okay, but he was hot, right?" Vonnie nudged me.

I sighed, reminded unwillingly of just how hot he was. But, beautiful face or not, he was still a vampire.

A freaking *vampire*.

"Yes, he was hot." And a vampire. "Mysterious." Like... *really* mysterious. "Nice body." Too bad about the *drinking blood* thing.

"What did he look like?" Vonnie asked, her chin resting on her pale hands. "Details, girl. You're letting the side down."

I sighed. "About five-foot-ten or eleven, dark, floppy hair, English accent. Face that should be on a piece of Roman statuary somewhere."

She blinked at me. "And your date was only ten minutes long, because…?"

"He's trouble," I said softly.

Vonnie regarded me with a serious expression for a moment. "The best ones are always trouble, Zorah."

I shook my head, though. "No. He's the kind of trouble that… I don't know if I could get out of afterward." *At least, not alive*, I finished silently.

But goddamn it, fool that I was—part of me still wanted to try. Just… not for the reason Vonnie probably assumed.

Six

"You're really harshing my vibe here, Zorah," Vonnie observed.

I snorted, dragging myself away from my grim musings. "Sorry, Von," I told her. "I can make up some story for you about a quickie in the Studio 88 restroom if you'd like, but the truth is, I don't have his number, he doesn't have mine, and I don't even know what his last name is. I'm pretty sure that means it's not going anywhere."

"He at least knows where you work," Vonnie said optimistically. "That's something, right?"

Yeah, it was something. I really wished I knew *what*.

"Maybe," I said.

You're stalking me, I'd accused, and he'd said, *a bit, yes*. He'd called me an enigma, because of my blood, then seemed to lose all interest when he'd realized I was telling the truth about not knowing what the hell he was talking about. How much could a vampire tell about you from drinking your blood?

After the meeting, I had even more questions, with no good answers and no way to track down the man who had them. I frowned. Wait, I did have one thing. I had the name Guthrie Leonides. I resolved to Google the hell out of that name as soon as I got off work this afternoon. Now, though, I'd just had a fresh crock of shit tipped into my lap in the form of this state auditor's bizarre accusations, and I had less than two hours to try and sort it out before I needed to leave for AJ's.

"Look, I need to try to figure out what's going on with these filings," I told Vonnie, who nodded her understanding and let me be.

I sat down at my desk and rifled through the papers, reorganizing them into some semblance of order. Some would be of use for the meeting tomorrow and some wouldn't. I pulled out manila folders for those I thought would help and filed away the rest.

After spending well over an hour recalculating and double-checking the paperwork, I still couldn't see any mistakes. I read through the message Daisy forwarded to me, went through every filing discrepancy the auditor named in the email, but not one of them looked out of place on my end. Beyond that, there wasn't much else I could do, so I organized the files in a box and brought them to Daisy.

"Here's all the supporting documentation. I honestly can't find anything I did wrong," I said, handing her the files. "I have no idea what your auditor guy is looking at on his end, but I'll be happy to come in tomorrow and talk to him face to face about it."

Daisy sighed and nodded. "Okay. Listen, I'm sorry I snapped at you. It's just, we can't afford to have the Department of Revenue crawling all over us. That's the kind of thing that destroys not-for-profits."

I smiled, reassuring her that I wasn't upset at all. "I know. It's okay. Really. I'm confident the mistake is on their end. It's probably something super simple."

"I hope so. Thanks for your help today," Daisy said, sounding tired. "See you tomorrow?"

I nodded, dreading the idea of another early morning—one where I would have to put on a cheerful face in front of powerful strangers. "Yep. Bright and early."

I left her office and grabbed my things, walking the few blocks to AJ's. The rain had stopped, though the wind was wicked crazy today. It would probably storm later in the afternoon. St. Louis at this time of year was thunderstorm and tornado territory, and there was a certain heavy humidity today that seemed undaunted by the wind. That kind of feeling in the atmosphere usually meant trouble.

A block away from AJ's, my vamp radar was up and running at full force. Unlikely though it was, I was hoping to run into Rans skulking around the restaurant. Of course, he wasn't there. That would have been way too easy, and my luck didn't seem to be running that way these days.

After changing into my uniform, I walked out of the women's restroom—only to be cornered near the bar by Jake, a new bartender who'd started working at the restaurant a couple of weeks ago. My jaw tightened. Christ, the front doors weren't even open yet, and we were going to do this? This day was shaping up to be a real bitch.

"So, Zorah." Jake stood way too close, physically cornering me next to the drinks station. "When are you gonna let me take you out?"

From a purely aesthetic standpoint, Jake was a good-looking guy. Sandy brown hair, blue eyes. Every girl's dream of the wholesome boy next door, if the wholesome boy next door happened to be a pushy, entitled asshole. He'd been pretty relentless about his intentions toward me from the day he got out of training.

"I'm not interested, Jake." I pushed myself back into the corner, trying to gain space to duck around him, but he only pressed forward to follow. He was so close, it half-looked like he was going to try and kiss me, right there in the open.

"Aw, don't be that way, beautiful. What about this weekend?" He waggled his eyebrows.

Seriously… who *did* that?

"Working, sorry." My voice was flat. It didn't faze him.

He shook his head. "Nah… you're not on the schedule for Saturday," he said. "I checked."

"This isn't the only place I work, Jake." I narrowed my eyes.

"You can't work every day." He tilted his head, trying to call my bluff.

"Pretty much, every day," I said. "A girl's gotta eat."

Taking half a step back, Jake shook his head. He was still smiling, and I was caught between relief that things weren't about to turn ugly — this time, at least — and a sort of dull rage at myself for feeling relieved when I wasn't the one in the wrong.

Even now, he wouldn't let up. "Okay, well maybe one night after work? I could take you out for drinks, then drop you off at home. Since you don't have a car."

My jaw was starting to ache with the effort of holding a neutral expression on my face. "I have a car. It's just in the shop right now." *Waiting for twenty-five hundred dollars to miraculously materialize.*

I might as well have been talking to a wall. "Cool, well you know you want to, so… soon. 'Kay?"

"I'm not interested, Jake. I have to get to work now. Can you… I don't know, maybe let me out of this corner?" I widened my eyes, waiting for him to get the message.

"Oh yeah, sure." He grinned wide, showing off his straight, white teeth. "Sorry, babe."

He shifted a couple of inches to the left, leaving just enough space that if I tried to squeeze past, I'd be brushing up against him.

"Dude." I stared him in the eyes. "You are seriously toeing the line with me right now, and I'm not in the mood for it."

The boy next door's face hardened, and I braced for whatever might come next. The dull rage from earlier was still churning in my gut, growing hot, wanting an outlet even though any outlet I could give it right now would probably end up being a clusterfuck. The kind of clusterfuck that ended up with me either unemployed, or sexually assaulted, or both.

Len—one of the line cooks—walked past on his way to the kitchen and halted abruptly, his eyes taking in the scene.

"Don't be a douche, Jake. What the hell are you doing? Back the fuck off of the poor woman."

When Jake didn't move immediately, Len narrowed his eyes and strode closer. He was taller than Jake, though not as broad through the chest and shoulders. That said, he also had an air of the bad boy about him that was reinforced by a purple fauxhawk, two full sleeves of tattoos, and an overabundance of facial piercings—nose, eyebrow, and lip. He usually hid out in the kitchen, but he obviously wasn't one to let a woman be bullied on his watch.

He also made the *best* steaks.

It wasn't that I couldn't handle guys like Jake, but right now, I wasn't going to lie—I was relieved Len was there. Especially when a flash of real anger passed over Jake's expression, bouncing between Len and me.

"Yeah, okay." Jake pursed his lips and raked his gaze down my body. He backed up a couple of steps then gestured to the side, ushering me to move. "Your loss, girl."

Averting my eyes from his irritated glare, I stepped past him and mouthed a thank you to Len as I walked over to my station and waited for customers entering the lobby to be seated.

Len shot me a tight smile and disappeared into the kitchen, while Jake went to stand behind the bar. I cursed the way my heart was pounding with adrenaline and tried to put on my game face for the customers. I didn't know what it said about me that I was more freaked out over the past five minutes than I had been by the revelation that vampires existed.

The hostesses were seating patrons out front, so I went out and did my job. By the time the lunch rush came and went, I'd made a good amount in tips, but my whole body was in pain. For whatever reason, there were a ton of lunch meetings today, and holding trays with lots of heavy plates on them had begun to take its toll. *Stupid joints and muscles. Why couldn't they just work the way they were supposed to?*

Some days, I really did feel like the oldest twenty-six-year-old alive.

After taking my first break, I got back on the floor. One of my new customers was a man sitting alone, dressed in a brown business suit that didn't complement his natural coloring at all.

I pulled out my order pad and walked up to his table.

"Good afternoon," I said. "I'll be your server today. What can I get started for you?"

There was something… strange about him. Off. He looked almost… unearthly? Was that the right word? Like he didn't belong here. Sort of shiny and golden, and too perfect to be real. He had long, blond hair that was tied back in a ponytail but his eyes… they were a strange shade of green. They caught me off guard, and I realized I was staring. The shade couldn't possibly be natural. They had to be contacts or something.

"I'll take an order of escargot with some garlic butter, to start."

Blinking back to myself, I tore my gaze away and wrote down the order: slimy snails and smelly butter. Not too many orders of escargot came out of our kitchen. In fact, I'd always wondered why the owners bothered to keep it on the menu when no one ordered it. "Will that be it for starters?" I asked. "A drink, maybe?"

"Hmm…I'll have a cognac. And a glass of water, with lemon."

Again, odd order.

While his facial features were overtly magnificent, for some reason he still repelled me on an instinctual level I couldn't explain. I felt like something was heaving inside me, screaming to run away. But that was stupid. I was just freaked out after the ugly scene with Jake earlier. That had to be it.

It was weird. Yesterday, a vampire was in here, and I could barely keep a lid on my fascination. Today, this guy— just as handsome and unusual, though in a different way—was making my skin crawl so badly I wanted to scratch furrows in my arms to make the sensation stop.

I was staring at him again. The guy cleared his throat and gave me the strangest look. Like I was being judged and indicted without a trial, ready for the sentence to be handed down.

Run, little girl, that look said. *Run as far and as fast as you can. The hunt is coming for you, and we will not be denied.*

Seven

"Tell me your name," the man commanded, his green eyes hard.

Never in my life could I recall feeling as disgusted by the proximity of another human being as I did at that moment. My stomach was curdling and my flesh felt like it was being burned off my bones under the intensity of his gaze.

"*Your name*," he repeated, his voice like iron.

Lifting my finger, I pointed mutely at my nametag.

Because, *duh*.

I watched him warily, trying to get a handle on my reaction. There was something... inherently repugnant about the man. It was the strangest feeling, like something in my body chemistry or my DNA was rejecting being in his presence.

The man lifted an eyebrow at my less than respectful response. "Has anybody ever told you that in Spanish, *zorra* means both a female fox and a promiscuous woman?"

It was not the first time I'd ever heard that line before—a line which, ironically, was not funny whatsoever given my abject failure in the 'being a sex kitten' department. Having gone through a high school Spanish class, as well as having dated a Latino boyfriend for all of two weeks, that particular pun had been played out years ago. And this dude obviously never considered that maybe—just maybe—I'd heard that one a time or two in my life?

"I'll go put in your appetizer order," I said tightly, walking away as fast as my feet would take me.

I felt like a magnet being repelled by another magnet. It was bad enough that I even tried getting another server to take over the table. Ponytail Guy stared at me shamelessly the whole time, never taking his gaze from me while I was visible from the seating area. No matter where I was on the floor, I felt my skin heating up, crawling, climbing over my bones, trying to get away.

It was almost physically painful.

I'd managed to get one of the other servers to bring out his drink, but when his food was ready, she was on break, so I reluctantly put the plates on a tray and brought them to his table. Placing the order in front of him, I did my damnedest to avoid eye contact at all costs.

"Thank you," he said, trying to sound pleasant although his voice raked over me like shards of glass. "So, tell me, Zorah. Do you live around here?"

I didn't want to give him any real answers, but, c'mon. Seriously. It didn't take a brain surgeon to figure that one out. "Well, I work here so… yeah?"

"Tell me about yourself." He laid his hands in his lap. Smiled. He was clearly trying to be conversational. Trying, and not caring that he was failing miserably.

My creeper radar was on full alert. Dear god, this day could not be over soon enough.

"I'm sorry, sir," I managed through gritted teeth. "I have other tables to attend to."

I started to walk away, but a hand like a steel band closed around my arm. I gasped and jerked free with a twisting move learned in some long-ago self-defense class. Heart pounding, I whirled, standing a step out of reach.

His flat green eyes were still peeling back the layers of my skin. "I'd like to know you better."

Visions of making a scene and getting fired warred with scenes of being kidnapped and chained up in Ponytail Guy's basement.

"I'm flattered," I choked out, "but I need to work."

I forced a smile that felt more like a rictus, and fled. For a while, I was able to get other servers to occasionally check on him, but he eventually pulled over the manager and told him I was neglecting him, so I got reamed and eventually slunk back over.

"Can I get those out of your way?" I asked cautiously, pointing at his empty plates.

He slid them across the table toward me. "How old are you, Zorah?"

"Twenties," I muttered, hoping giving him something unimportant would get him to lay off. It didn't.

"What about your parents. Are they alive?"

I froze at his question. Why would he ask that? The way he looked at me, it was as though he already knew the answers to every question he asked. Like he could see right into my head, and sense my dislike of him. Like he already knew things about me that I didn't even know about myself.

Who the hell was this guy? Why was I suddenly ground zero for weirdness?

I tried to defuse the situation while shutting him down at the same time. "Listen, I'm not comfortable giving personal information to a man I don't know. I'm sure you can understand that."

"Bring me an order of tiramisu, Zorah. And another drink." He set his glass at the edge of the table.

I nodded, grabbing the dirty dishes and his glass. "Fine, I'll bring it right out."

As I walked back to the kitchen, I could feel him staring.

Watching.

Hours passed, and Creepy Ponytail Guy stayed.

He freaking *stayed*. Ordering drinks to placate management and keep from getting thrown out. The entire damn time, his stare followed me everywhere. Table to table. Floor to kitchen. It didn't matter what I was doing — he was always watching.

Three o'clock finally came and my shift ended. I was so freaked out that I was physically shaking, too afraid to even walk to the bus stop alone. Times like this, I really wished my car wasn't in the shop. Though to be fair, I probably wasn't in any shape to drive safely.

I hid in the kitchen, chewing on my thumbnail, frazzled by the creeper sitting in my section. *Still.*

Any pride I might have had was long gone as I waited for Len to finish what he was doing.

"Hey Len," I began, a bit hesitant. "You're off now, right?"

Len pulled the hairnet off his head, his purple fauxhawk springing to life as if it hadn't been squashed beneath a net for hours. Len was a sweetheart under all the bad boy trappings, from what I knew of him. He'd always been nice to me, and after the scene with Jake this morning, I felt a lot more comfortable with him.

"Yeah, I'm finished here. What's up, Zorah?" He washed his hands at the sink along the back wall, then untied the apron he was wearing and tossed it into the laundry bin a few feet away.

I was suddenly very glad he was here.

Taking a steadying breath, I said, "Would you mind driving me home? There's this creepy guy who's been in my section for hours now, asking me personal questions. Like, *hours*. Seriously. He's still here, and frankly I'm afraid to leave alone."

Len frowned, the ring in his eyebrow glinting. "I'd be happy to, only I didn't drive. I live, like, four blocks down."

"Oh." I deflated as I peered out toward the floor.

"How'd you get here?" Len asked.

"I took the bus." God, I was really starting to hate that damned bus.

"What happened to your car? Didn't you have a little red Civic?"

"Transmission went out. They said it's gonna be at least a couple thousand to fix it." I shrugged. "I'm still figuring that out."

He nodded in sympathy. "Yeah, I hear you. I don't even have a car. Fortunately, everything I need is within walking distance." He looked at me for a minute, clearly taking note of my fear. "Don't worry, sweetheart. I'll get you home safe. Bus stop's just a few blocks away. What about the Metro?"

I shook my head. "I have a pass, but there's not a stop near my house, so I've been stuck taking the bus instead."

"Listen, I'll walk you to the bus stop and sit with you till it comes," Len said. "What table's this creep at?"

"Twenty-one."

Len held up a finger, silently warning me to stay put as he walked to the edge of the seating area and scoped out the situation. "The blonde with the ponytail?" he asked.

I nodded. "He's still there, then? Jesus, I've been off the floor for, like, twenty minutes now. I'm seriously freaking out here." I ran my fingers through my hair, agitated. "What the fuck does he want from me?"

"I dunno, girl, but he's on my radar now. I've got your back."

"Thanks, Len."

"It's nothing," he said. "Grab your shit, and let's get you home."

I wasted no time grabbing my backpack from my locker. Len walked me out the employee door, through the alley and down the street to the nearest bus stop, which was barely half a block away. After the short walk to the stop, we sat on the bench under the grimy shelter for about fifteen minutes waiting for the next bus.

I couldn't keep my nerves at bay, constantly watching, expecting the creeper guy to make an appearance. Len was a solid presence at my side.

"Thanks, Len." I stood as the bus pulled up and dug into my bag to get my bus pass, telling myself that once I was on board, I was safe. For some reason, I didn't believe it. "I'll... see you tomorrow?"

Len shook his head. "No, I'm coming with you. You're about to jump out of your own skin."

A hint of warmth blossomed in my chest. "You really don't have to do that."

He shook his head. "Yes, I do. I want to make sure you get home okay. I promised, remember?"

Some of the tension flowed out of me. "Thank you, Len. That means a lot to me." I smiled. It really did.

He quirked a crooked smile in return and ushered me up the steps. "It's no thing. Let's just get you home." He pulled cash out of his pocket and paid the bus fare as we got on, then walked back and sat beside me for the ride.

"Where do you live, anyway?" he asked.

"South City. Off Hampton. You?"

"I share a loft with my boyfriend downtown. He's a chef at Le Grand Concours."

I lifted my eyebrows. Le Grand Concours was a sweet gig, if you could get it. "Nice." *Not to men-*

tion, proof that most of the good ones were batting for the other team.

"Here, give me your phone," Len said, gesturing.

"Okay." I pulled my phone out of my bag and unlocked it, then handed it over.

"This is my phone number, all right?" He got to the contacts and entered his number. "If you ever need anything, let me know. And hey, I only live a few blocks from AJ's. So I can walk you to the bus stop anytime."

My smile widened. "Thanks, Len."

The bus arrived at my stop, which was only a couple of blocks from my house. The street I lived on was quiet, so the walk home wouldn't be too terrifying.

"I mean it," Len reiterated. "If you need anything, give me a call."

I nodded as I stood to get off the bus. "I will. Thanks for making a shitty day less shitty, Len. I'll see you tomorrow." I got off and waved at him as it drove away from my stop.

The two-block walk home was blissfully uneventful, and I made it without any other incident. As I stepped onto my front porch, my phone dinged. It was Len, checking up on me. I smiled as I texted back that I was walking in the front door and locking it behind me. Then I told him to tell his boyfriend from me that he was one lucky dude.

The lock clicked behind me. *Home.*

I sat on my couch and for the first time all day, I could breathe.

What a terrible day. After all that, I desperately needed a drink. And a bath. I could still feel that guy's bad mojo crawling over me, like spiders. After balancing my need to relax against the damage that a glass or two of hard cider would do to my already shaky health, I said fuck it and poured some for myself. I took a few sips and wandered into the bathroom to fill the tub. When it was steaming, I stripped and tiptoed in, cider by my side and soft music playing in the background.

I closed my eyes and tried to relax. The mountains of bubbles over hot water went some way toward washing off the invisible layer of grime left by my interactions with that horrible man, as well as soothing my sore, tired muscles.

Still, nine o'clock tomorrow morning would come sooner than I wanted it to, and as hard as I tried, I couldn't relax completely. When the water started to cool, I got out and spent some time looking up Guthrie Leonides on my phone. He seemed to be a pretty big deal in business circles—bigger than I would have guessed based on his straightforward, laid-back demeanor. I jotted down a few notes, and tried a search for his name and Rans together. No results.

That avenue exhausted, I killed the rest of the evening mentally organizing my arguments for the meeting with the auditor in the morning. I dared to hope that it wouldn't be nearly as big a deal as Daisy seemed to think. I'd gone over the material listed in the email thoroughly, and I was confident that I was in the right.

After a late dinner and an hour or so spent trying to slow my racing mind with a thoroughly forgettable romance novel, I popped another handful of painkillers and headed off to bed. Predictably, my aches and pains combined with unsettling images from the day to leave me tossing and turning for a long time before I finally slipped into to a restless sleep.

My recurring dream came shortly thereafter.

It was hot outside, and the sun was summer-bright. It illuminated the colorful banners and bunting hanging around the stage. Red. White. Blue. The crowd was happy, cheering. At first, I could only see legs, like tree trunks in the forest where Mommy and Daddy took me camping sometimes.

Then, Daddy lifted me and I had the best view ever, sitting on his shoulders. His strong hands steadied me as both of us watched Mommy talking on stage. Mommy was going to be a Senator. I didn't know what that was exactly, but it was a real important job. She was gonna help loads of people, and be famous, like a movie star.

That made sense, because she was already pretty like a movie star. Daddy and me were so proud of her.

She was talking now, lifting a hand when people around us started cheering again. But behind us, someone yelled. It wasn't a happy noise like the others. I tried to twist around and look, not liking how that yell made me feel. Now other people were yelling, screaming, and Daddy whirled around. Then he was grabbing me… pulling me down from his shoulders… wrapping his body around me.

I saw Mommy for a moment before I was surrounded by Daddy's body, jostled by people running past us. Mommy was frowning, her eyes wide as she met mine. I saw her mouth open before I lost sight of her.

A loud noise like fireworks hurt my ears, and more people were screaming, running, crying. I started crying, too. Mommy said we'd watch fireworks later, but why was everyone so scared? Why were the fireworks starting now, when it was light out and Mommy was trying to talk?

"Oh, god," Daddy was saying. "Oh god—no, no, no."

He hoisted me up, holding me against his hip, and then he was running, too. Shoving against the crowd that was trying to run the other way.

"Sasha! *Sasha!*" He was screaming Mommy's name, and I sobbed louder, afraid because I didn't know what was happening.

"Mommy!" I cried, the noise eaten by the louder noises all around me.

Daddy climbed up on the stage, dragging me with him. His hands hurt where they were gripping me too hard. Mommy was lying on the ground on her back, like that one time she slipped on the ice last winter and fell down. But this time, she wasn't laughing and saying, "Ow, ow, ow, stupid ice!"

She wasn't saying anything at all. She was just staring at the sky, lying in the middle of a big red puddle spreading around her, red stains on her blouse. Her skirt.

Everywhere.

Her chest had a big ugly hole in it. Dad dropped me to the stage. Someone else picked me up and covered my eyes.

But it was too late. I already saw.

My mommy was dead.

Eight

At first, I thought the sound of my alarm going off was the sound of wailing sirens in my dream. When my brain untangled reality from nightmare, I jerked awake, lunging upright in bed. I was breathing hard, my heart racing so fast that my chest hurt.

I stared at the gray light of dawn barely illuminating my childhood bedroom, some distant part of my mind recognizing the panic attack for what it was. It had been a while, but I knew this feeling far too well. I knew that I wasn't strong enough to pull myself out of it by willpower alone. I just had to weather it and hope that this wouldn't be the time that I truly had a heart attack or a stroke.

The only way out was through.

I sat in bed shaking, hugging my knees, feeling like I couldn't get enough air as images of the hole in my mother's chest superimposed with images of the hole in Rans' chest. *Rans was alive*, I tried to tell myself. *Well, maybe not alive, exactly, but he was okay*. I'd seen him afterward. Talked to him. Felt the brush of his fingers against my cheek.

None of that makes your mom any less dead, said the horrible little voice that lived inside me.

"It was a long time ago," I whispered to the empty room, finally getting my breath back as reality asserted itself. "Twenty years."

God, I was backsliding. I'd been hanging on pretty well these past few years. Making it. Managing my various physical and mental challenges well enough to cope, day by day. I didn't want to return to this place of being broken and useless. Damaged goods.

And it had all started two days ago, when a vampire chose my shed to break into. Was all of this happening now because Rans had drunk my blood?

I wanted nothing more than to chug every bottle of hard cider in my fridge and pull the blankets over my head until everything went away, but that would be the worst possible thing for me to do on so many levels. I told myself that it would be like giving up, and I wasn't a goddamned quitter.

The red display on the bedside alarm clock read six-thirty, and I had to meet the auditor at MMHA at nine. In fact, I should get there early so I could get all the files ready to go. I couldn't huddle here on my bed like the terrified six-year-old that still lived inside me, buried deep.

Food. Ibuprofen. Stretching exercises. Shower. Get dressed. Leave.

It was no different than any of the other rough mornings I'd had in the past few years. Power through, don't give up, and eventually things would get better. I eased out of bed, feeling joints creak and pop, feeling my gut churn. Outside, rain spattered against the window, the atmosphere heavy and gray.

━━━━◆━━━━

At fifteen minutes until nine, I hurried toward the glass doors leading into MMHA, wincing as my body protested. The skies opened just as I ducked under the awning, and I sighed in relief. I might be a walking disaster in most respects, but in this, at least, my timing had been impeccable.

The moment I stepped across the threshold, my heart sped up as I realized that, impeccable timing or not, I'd just stepped into a nightmare to rival the one I'd woken from a couple of hours ago.

I'd thought yesterday was bad? *Surprise, Zorah!* Today had just been fucked twice as badly. Adrenaline rushed through my veins as I saw Creepy Ponytail Guy standing in the office, talking to Daisy and a few other members of the board. There were people here that I hadn't seen since they accepted my volunteer application. There were others I'd never met at all, wearing suits and serious expressions. These were people involved in executive decision making, not day-to-day operations.

Why were they here now? This was supposed to be a low-key, informal meeting to straighten out whatever mix-up or misunderstanding had the Department of Revenue's panties in a twist. Not a full-blown gathering of the board of directors.

As soon as Daisy saw me, her eyes narrowed. Anger clouded her expression.

There was something off-kilter about the atmosphere in the office. Daisy didn't seem like herself. She didn't normally do cold anger. She did short, explosive bouts of temper that blew over quickly and were inevitably followed by an apology.

This morning, she walked over to me, her face unsmiling. She looked like a completely different person than the one I'd left yesterday. It was like we were strangers. Like I didn't know her at all.

"Conference room," she said coldly. "*Now*. Mr. Werther from the state auditor's office wants to speak with you."

"What's the board doing here?" I asked. My voice was shaking.

"You've messed up royally, Zorah." Her expression never thawed. "There are going to be repercussions. Serious ones."

My breathing was speeding up, another panic attack threatening. "No, but I showed you…"

Daisy cut me off. "I don't want to hear it. Tell it to the board."

I stood there, my mouth open, staring at Daisy. At the board members filing into the conference room. At the creeper from the restaurant. His eyes met mine, a slow smile spreading over his too-perfect face.

My skin started crawling again, even worse than it had yesterday. On top of feeling like total shit, I now felt like I was going to throw up. If I did, I made a mental note to aim my stomach contents in Ponytail Guy's direction.

Everyone was inside the conference room at that point except me. I grew faint, beads of clammy sweat breaking out on my forehead. It felt like it was about a hundred degrees in the office. I took in a breath, let it out slowly, then went over to the small refrigerator in the corner and pulled out a bottle of water. I suspected I was going to need it to get through this meeting.

I mentally reviewed the filings as I stood gathering myself to go in. Everything had been done correctly. I'd double and triple checked it yesterday. It was all in order. I saw absolutely no errors, and sure as hell not the ones this guy was claiming I had made. Not to mention, I wasn't the last person to look at the non-profit's paperwork before it was filed.

MMHA had an oversight committee. I was just a lowly volunteer. I wasn't solely responsible for keeping the books, and someone was always supposed to check up on my work. Even if I'd missed something, someone higher up the food chain should have noticed and fixed it, or at least flagged it. If they hadn't, was that really my fault?

Trying to shake off my burgeoning panic, I carried the bottle of water and my backpack into the conference room. It wasn't a huge room to begin with, but right now with twelve people crammed inside, it felt like a sardine box. Claustrophobia joined the clamoring chorus of reasons to lose my shit. As soon as I set down my backpack next to the last remaining chair, the room fell silent. Everyone stared at Ponytail Guy, including Daisy. It was like they were following his lead, waiting for permission to speak. Permission to fucking *breathe*.

Ponytail Guy leaned back in his chair, regarding me coolly. "I am Caspian Werther of the Missouri State Auditor's office. Explain how you came up with the numbers for Form 990-T."

I narrowed my eyes, unfamiliar with that form. "Can I see the files?"

"You already have the files. Explain why there is more than seventy-two thousand dollars missing from this organization's withholdings and why your name displays on withdrawal slips at the bank."

I stared at him. He might as well have been speaking a foreign language. "What? I don't..."

He cut me off. "Do you understand that Form 26B relates to for-profit organizations and that by filing such form, you are in violation of Missouri law?" Werther's eyes narrowed. He tilted his chin down, staring at me just like he had yesterday.

Looking right through me.

"I never filed that form," I said. "Why would I? I need to see the documentation." I looked to Daisy and gestured, waiting for her to hand me the box of files I'd given her yesterday. The files that showed I had filled out the proper forms and that I had done nothing wrong.

Daisy looked at Werther, who shook his head almost imperceptibly in the negative.

She returned her gaze to me, crossed her arms over her chest and shook her head as he had. "I can't do that."

The sense of unreality grew. "How am I supposed to defend myself if you won't even let me see the files?"

"We didn't bring you here to defend yourself," Werther said. "Simply to admit that you have been embezzling money from this non-profit. The evidence is clear."

"*What*?" My eyes went wide. Where was this even *coming* from? I tried to regroup. "I have never touched a dime of MMHA's money. *Ever*." My heart was beating so hard that my chest was aching again. I felt as though I was in real danger of throwing up. "I've never even handled the money at this place. I just crunch numbers and fill out forms!"

"You committed fraud," Werther said. "They trusted you."

Daisy stood up, pointing at me with a shaking finger. "How could you take money from us?" She sounded appalled, like she believed everything Werther was saying without question. "You're a fraud. We trusted you!"

After Daisy started, so did a few of the other board members.

All yelling out that I'd committed fraud. That I'd embezzled money. That they'd trusted me.

Like drones, they repeated every word he said.

I felt my grip on reality slipping. Was I in some kind of alternate universe? What in the *actual fuck* was going on here?

Every new lie that spewed from Werther's mouth was immediately picked up by Daisy and the other board members. It was as though he had some kind of mental hold over them. Like they couldn't think for themselves anymore.

Like Werther had somehow compelled them to believe whatever he said.

I had volunteered at this place for years. *Years.* But these people—people I knew, and who knew me—were all acting like I was a complete stranger that had walked into their office and stolen money at gunpoint.

Some of the board members started spewing things that were completely crazy. Saying I lived in a fancy house, leeching money from MMHA, when in fact I lived in a crappy 1940s two-bedroom bungalow that I could only afford because my dad had refinanced the mortgage for me. Claiming I drove an expensive car when everyone in the office knew I had a broken down Civic, and had needed to take the damn bus to even be here today.

Standing in front of them all, people I'd respected and trusted, I fought back tears, only the growing sense of dissociation with reality making it possible for me to keep them inside.

"Stop!" I said it aloud, though the croaked word was swallowed up by the growing clamor of outrage in the room. This entire thing was off-the-wall crazy. I refused to stay here any longer, accused of doing terrible things while Caspian Werther stared at me like some kind of mildly interesting science experiment.

I flung my backpack over my shoulder and glared at him.

"I don't know who you are or how you pulled this off, but you won't get away with this," I said, pitching my shaking voice to be heard over the din.

Werther smiled. "Won't I? I daresay I'll be seeing you again soon, Zorah Bright. Until then."

Daisy blocked my approach to the conference room door, her face the same cold mask it had been earlier. "You're fired. I don't ever want to see your face here again. Do you understand me?"

That broke me.

A horrible choking, clawing sensation clogged my throat. I opened the conference room door and rushed out wordlessly, passing Vonnie as I hurried by.

"Zorah?" Vonnie called my name, but I couldn't speak. "What happened? Where are you going?"

There was no way I could answer her. I had to get out of this place before I lost it. Before that Werther guy came after me—because even though I wanted to believe this was the end of it, after his final words to me, something in my gut knew the nightmare was far from over. When I left the building, it was pouring outside. I didn't care. I just ran, as far and as fast as I could. It had been a long time since I'd run like that, but I didn't know what else to do. I'd had enough. At that point, my body was in agony and my spirits were drowned.

I just wanted to go home.

About a block from where my lungs gave out, I saw a bus stop through the rain. I staggered up to it and sat, wet and alone, waiting for the bus to come. That was when I broke down crying.

Everything I'd spent the past few years working towards at MMHA was gone. Part of me had hoped the volunteer work would lead somewhere bigger, but if it didn't I was okay with that. All I'd wanted was to do something good and make a difference.

Even that had turned into a disaster.

Fifteen minutes later, my tears were somewhat under control. The bus finally came. Unfortunately, it was the wrong bus line, so I ended up riding it much longer than I expected to. Lucky for me, my phone was fully charged. I dragged a pair of earbuds from my backpack and tried to drown out the thoughts in my brain with the loudest, angriest music I could find.

It didn't work, but at least I'd be home soon, where I could crawl into bed and hide from the world. Hell, maybe I'd even call in sick tomorrow at AJ's. I didn't care anymore. All I wanted to do was sleep. After way too long riding around on unfamiliar buses, I finally caught the right one and made it to my stop.

I was soaked, but the rain suited my state of mind. Thanks to the overcast skies, it was far darker than it should have been at midday. That, too, suited my state of mind.

I got off the bus a couple of blocks from my house. When I turned toward my street, I saw a bunch of flashing red and blue lights in my neighborhood. My overworked heart started hammering again, wondering what the hell was happening now. Had there been a fire? Had one of my neighbors called an ambulance? As I reached the corner, it hit me.

It wasn't the fire service or an ambulance — it was the police. Lots of them. And they weren't just *near* my house. They were surrounding it.

I started to panic. Any other day, I would have assumed that it was just some stupid misunder-standing. I would have approached the police cars and asked what was going on. But today? No. This wasn't a coincidence.

It wasn't paranoia when they really were out to get you. And whoever this Werther guy was, he was out for blood. *Mine.*

I remembered my dream — the one about Mom. Her death. How all these years, I'd suspected it wasn't an accident. Now, I was more certain than ever. Something was wrong in the world. Terribly, terribly wrong.

I could feel it in the ache of my bones. The frantic beat of my heart. Werther wanted me, and I needed to run far and fast. I thought about the creeping sensation of dread he engendered in me, and knew that I couldn't let him catch me. Some-thing deep inside me was screaming that letting him catch me would mean death, or worse.

Taking a deep breath, I pulled the fallen hood of my raincoat over my head and kept walking. Past the corner, past my street, past the police cars waiting for me. One step at a time, I walked like I didn't have a care in the world. The rain beat down harder — a fitting accompaniment to my life being washed away in the space of a single morning. I was soaked — a drowned rat scurrying for safety — but at least I was still free.

At least I wasn't in Werther's hands.

About a mile away from my house stood a convenience store with a small deli attached. I glanced over my shoulder, seeing no indication anyone was following me. In the pit of my stomach, though, I knew they'd be looking soon. Coming after me.

As I got closer to my temporary destination, my mind spun with worry. I'd watched enough police procedural shows to know all the ways they could track a person these days. Was there any way to hide from this, if Werther really wanted to find me? Especially if he had the cops in his pocket somehow?

Finally, I reached the entrance to the little sandwich shop. Breathless from exhaustion and panic, I scanned the interior for anybody suspicious. Not that I'd know what *suspicious* looked like under these circumstances, but everything seemed normal. Nothing set off my internal radar. It wasn't a particularly busy day, and only two other people were inside eating.

I grabbed a cheap plastic booth in the corner and buried my head in my arms. I tried holding in the fresh round of tears, but I couldn't do it. I was tired. Wet. Alone. I didn't know what to do. Who to call. Who to trust.

When I could breathe again, I lifted my head. The kid at the counter was eyeing me warily, but thankfully she didn't seem inclined to come over and talk to me. I wiped my face with a napkin and tried to take stock. A quick rummage through my backpack unearthed a twenty-dollar bill, my Metro pass, and a credit card that was about a hundred dollars from being maxed out.

I cast about for anyone I could call. Vonnie was a no-go because of the MMHA connection. I thought she'd seemed okay when I'd rushed past her while making my escape. But if Daisy could be turned into a pod person, Vonnie could be, too.

My breath caught as an idea surfaced. *Len.* I could call Len. He'd given me his number yesterday, and for some reason he seemed to give a damn about me. When another nervous glance at my surroundings showed nothing suspicious, I pulled out my cell and scrolled to his number, then hit call and waited.

It rang a few times before Len finally answered. *"Who's this?"* he asked, and I realized he'd have no way to recognize my number.

I swallowed hard. "Len? It's Zorah. I... I'm in trouble."

There was a slight pause. *"Oh, my god. What the hell is going on?"* His voice was a harsh whisper. *"Zorah, the cops are here at the restaurant, and they're asking about you."*

I had to suppress a moan of near-despair. "I didn't do anything, Len," I said, desperate to make him believe me. "They're at my house, too. I don't know what the hell is happening!"

Another pause. I held my breath. When Len spoke again, his voice held a faint tremor. *"Okay. Okay, Zorah. Whatever you do, don't come here. Look…*

they're coming back to the kitchen. I can't talk now. I'll try to call you in a few minutes. Be safe."

Len hung up and I tapped the *end* button, feeling the finality as the call disconnected. I sat in the booth, staring out the window — watching the rain fall to earth.

Nowhere to go. No one to trust.

Alone.

Nine

Numbness was starting to creep in around the fear, and I welcomed it. The girl at the counter was still giving me the side-eye. No surprise since I hadn't ordered anything, and had basically come in and started crying all over her freshly wiped table. I was also starting to get unwanted attention from the other patrons. Under the circumstances, having attention on me felt dangerous.

I'd managed to blot my tears and was trying to think through my options logically when Len called back. I nearly fumbled the phone in my haste to take the call.

"Len?" I asked breathlessly.

"Zorah, what the fuck happened today?" Len asked, his voice quiet. *"Tell me quick — the cops are out talking to the manager right now."*

I took a deep breath, trying to organize my rampaging thoughts. "Okay. Remember that stalker guy last night? Well, long story short — he claims to be a state auditor. I volunteer downtown at a non-profit and help with keeping their books. Ponytail Guy showed up this morning claiming I embezzled money from the organization and committed tax fraud to hide it. My boss fired me on the spot and when I went home, there were a bunch of cops surrounding my house. But I swear,

Len—I *swear* to you—I didn't do anything. You know me… would I be riding the bus and stressing over my busted transmission if I'd been skimming tens of thousands of dollars from someone? None of it makes any sense!"

There was a short pause. *"I believe you, Zorah."* I released my breath, taken by surprise at how much it affected me to hear someone say that. He continued, *"Look, if you didn't do anything… maybe you should just give yourself up. I mean, I'm not any huge fan of the cops or the legal system, but these things usually have a way of working themselves out if you're innocent."*

I shook my head even though he couldn't see it. "No, there's way more to this. I'm telling you, the stuff he asked me yesterday at the restaurant was all really personal. It had nothing to do with the non-profit or my work. And honestly, Len, the guy gives me the major creeps. It's not just the normal 'guys suck' thing, but like… he's danger-ous. Seriously fucking dangerous. I know, it sounds stupid. But whenever I'm around him, I want to crawl out of my own skin and run away."

Another pause. *"I saw how freaked out you were with him. And that was after seeing how freaked out you weren't, when Jake was being an asshole before your shift. I just… want you to keep your options open, when it comes to the police, okay? Other than that, are you safe?"*

"Yeah," I said unthinkingly. "I think so. I'm at the—"

He cut me off. *"No, stop. Don't tell me where you are. It's safer that way. In case the police… you know."*

Jesus. He was right. And I wasn't used to having to think like this. Like a fugitive. "Yeah, okay."

"Good. Hey, I've got to go. They're coming back into the kitchen again. Stay safe, girl."

The phone went silent. He'd hung up.

I was alone again. I shook my head. Who was I kidding? I was alone whether Len was on the phone with me or not. What did I expect him to do for me right now?

Cops were at AJ's looking for me. They were at my house. Who the hell knew where else they were, but they were obviously dead serious about finding me. I tried to think. I'd never been so much as fingerprinted before. I wasn't in any registry that I knew of, so they couldn't really know what I looked like unless they looked up my driver's license, right?

Even so, I wasn't at all sure of my ability to evade the cops on my own. If they wanted to find me badly enough, they would—eventually. But maybe I could stay out of the net long enough to get some legal help lined up, at the very least. Right now, if I disappeared, who would notice?

I didn't know if I could trust Vonnie, or if Werther might have gotten to her somehow. My supervisor at the restaurant would assume the cops had caught up with me. Len would know something was wrong, but it was a stretch to expect him to stick his neck out any further for me than he already had. I was growing to like him, but the reality was, we barely knew each other. It was a sobering thought.

I sat for a while longer, thinking about what I had with me. Twenty bucks and a credit card. Maybe I could find a cheap motel somewhere, but the cops could probably track me based on my credit card use. I really didn't know much about that stuff, beyond the fact that with technology today, if somebody wanted to find me, they would.

The more I thought about how to get out of this, the angrier I got. I was completely alone. No close friends, no family worth a damn. How the hell had my life come to this? I was not going to become some statistic… some kind of bullshit Illuminati conspiracy victim. This was America. People weren't supposed to be hauled away by the police on trumped-up charges to face god-knew-what at the hands of creepy government officials. I refused to lie down for this.

The counter girl was beginning to look decidedly twitchy. I figured it would be a good idea to relocate before she started to think about calling her manager or asking me to leave. There was a grocery store a few blocks away that would be much busier. I figured crowds would be my friend right now. Anonymity was what I needed.

Taking a deep breath, I stood and gathered my things, then left the deli. As I glanced around the area, there didn't seem to be anybody looking for me. Still, I didn't want to take any chances. I put my hood up as I started walking down the cracked sidewalk.

It was a busy street, so nobody would pay much mind to me… I hoped. But I kept my head down just in case. After a couple of blocks, I reached the grocery store and went inside. The pharmacy was beside the restrooms, and there were benches in the hallway outside. Sitting here, I would look like any other customer waiting for a prescription to be filled. The noise of tinny Muzak and people talking would cover the details of a quiet phone conversation, as long as no one decided to plop down on the same bench as me.

To discourage that, I set my bag down next to me, taking up way more space than I really needed. Still full of my earlier determination to do whatever it took to get out of this, I pulled my phone out, took a deep breath, and called my dad.

I could predict with reasonable certainty how this conversation was going to go. But the fact remained, he was the only resource I hadn't tried to use yet. Realistically, at this point, he was the only resource I had left.

After a few rings, he answered.

"Dad?" My hands were shaking just holding my cell.

"Zorah? Is that you? I'm working, what do you want?" Short. To the point. Exactly what I'd expected.

"Yeah, sorry. Listen, I really need you, Dad. Something's happened."

The phone went silent for a long moment. I seemed to be having that effect on people a lot today. Then, *"Are you okay? What is it?"*

Holy crap. Was that concern in his voice?

"No. I'm not okay, Dad. I need help." I couldn't lie, as much as I wanted to. As much as I wanted to pretend I was strong, and that I had my shit together, I really, *really* didn't right now. "Something real bad is going on, and I don't know what to do. Last night at AJ's, this creepy guy came in and harassed me for my entire shift—start to finish. He kept asking me things like if I lived in town, and how old I was. He even asked if you and Mom were alive."

My voice trembled on the last sentence. I took a deep breath and plunged ahead.

"Then today, I went to MMHA and the same guy was there, claiming to be an auditor for the state. He was saying that I embezzled money and committed fraud, which I swear to you I didn't. I had the supporting documents all ready to prove that I hadn't done anything wrong, but he wouldn't even let me defend myself. My supervisor fired me on the spot, and this guy threatened me on my way out. When I went home, there were cop cars surrounding the house, and a guy at AJ's told me over the phone that cops were there, too, looking for me. I'm so sorry to dump this on you, Dad... but I don't know what to do. I didn't know who else to call. I'm afraid. Really fucking afraid. What do I do?"

Finally, I ran out of breath and the tumbling words fell silent. I knew what came next, and tried to brace for it. *You've always been trouble. I told you something like this would happen eventually.*

When he spoke, I had to replay the words in my head to make sure I'd heard them properly.

"Find the nearest Western Union location to wherever you are right now. I'll wire you money anonymously so you can buy a bus ticket to Chicago."

Wait, what?

Stunned, I scrambled to phrase a reply. My father was organizing an escape plan… for me? This wasn't how our relationship worked. I'd hoped for, well, honestly I wasn't sure what I'd hoped for. Some kind of advice on finding a lawyer. Maybe an insight into how the Department of Revenue and the state auditor's office processed things like this.

Not… real help. Not *support*.

Damn it, I was going to burst into tears again. "Thank you," I breathed, my body feeling shaky.

He wasn't interested in heartfelt exchanges, though. *"Whatever you do, don't tell anyone who you are. Don't use credit cards, or ID. You won't need an ID to claim the money. They'll let you use a ten-digit code and a password in lieu of identification documents. I'll run down the street and get it set up on my end, then text the code to you."*

I was still in shock. "Okay," I said faintly.

"Afterward, you should head straight to the bus station downtown. Buy a ticket from St. Louis to Chicago with cash, and I'll meet you at the station when you get here."

This was so completely out of character for my dad, I couldn't help but freak out a little. Why was he helping me? Was he only a distant, passive-aggressive asshole when things were normal? But when shit got real, he suddenly turned into Super Dad, flying to the rescue? I was having real trouble wrapping my mind around the concept.

"Dad—" I began, unsure how the sentence would continue.

"I'll contact you from the Western Union store in a few minutes." And just like that, he hung up.

I stared at the phone. Did that really just happen? Did my dad just pull a solid to protect me? *My dad*? The man who'd emotionally checked out of our stunted, two-person family almost two decades ago?

I sat there staring around me at the bustling grocery store in the city I'd lived in all my life. A city I was about to leave, maybe never to return. Still fighting shock over this whole thing, I grabbed my backpack. There was a Western Union desk right at the customer service counter of the store. I'd walked past it a hundred times over the years, though I'd never had cause to use it before. I wondered if the store had a cheap prepaid phone I could buy, as well. It seemed like I should probably ditch mine as soon as possible, just to be safe.

As I walked from the pharmacy to the customer service desk, I wondered anew at my dad's actions. For twenty years, he'd played the part of a man who'd lost everything he cared about and just… given up. But maybe he still had something left to lose after all.

Me.

Ten

Waiting was slow torture. I imagined a hundred ways this could go wrong while I stood in line at the Western Union desk. The top of the list was Dad coming to his senses and changing his mind—refusing to answer his phone. Leaving me hanging. With only two people ahead of me, I picked up my cell and called him.

He picked up on the second ring. *"Zorah? I'm at the place now. Give me a minute to get the transfer set up."*

"Okay," I breathed, relief washing through me. He hadn't abandoned me. I waited, foot jittering as I listened to the indistinct sound of people talking over the tinny connection, too far away from the microphone for the sense of the words to come through. The last person in front of me finished their transaction and I stepped up to the desk.

"Here's the code and password. I'll just read it off rather than texting. That way I don't have to hang up." Dad rattled off the numbers and letters while I jotted them down on a scrap of paper. *"I'm sending you two hundred fifty dollars. Use some of it to buy a burner phone, then ditch yours. Be sure to take out the SIM card and cut it into bits."*

My dad seemed surprisingly good at being sneaky. I briefly wondered if he just watched a lot of television, or if there were things I didn't know about him.

"I thought of that," I assured him. "They've got prepaid phones here. I'll get a couple, just to be safe. Thanks, Dad. I really mean that. I don't know what I would've—"

"It's all right." His voice was shaky, probably as shaky as mine was. *"Be careful, Zorah. No more phone calls on this phone. Dump it and destroy the SIM card like I told you."* The line was silent for a second before he let out a breath. *"And Zorah…?"*

"Yeah, Dad?"

"I love you."

The line went silent, and then he was gone.

My dad hadn't said he loved me in years. In fact, I couldn't even remember the last time the words left his lips.

Fuck.

I filled out the paperwork with unshed tears clogging my throat, and handed everything back to the lady. After that, I had to wait for her to check that it was in order and process the transfer. Another ten minutes, and I had the wired money in hand. I purchased a couple of cheap flip phones and a prepaid card that had talk and text on it, along with a pair of scissors.

Transferring the important names and numbers over to the new phones only took a couple of minutes. There were depressingly few of them. Then I took the SIM card out of my old phone and stuffed it into my back pocket. Returning to the restrooms, I sat in a stall and sliced the tiny plastic and metal wafer into the thinnest shreds I could manage. Some of the shreds went in the trashcan next to the sink. The others I would throw in random trashcans on the way to the station.

Unsure how much the ticket to Chicago would be, I used a few dollars to buy some food and a drink. When I was done eating, I left the store and paid cash for bus fare to the St. Louis Gateway Transportation Center, where the Greyhound station and Amtrak terminal were located.

The only seats on the bus were near the front. As the driver headed along the meandering route toward the station, he talked to himself. He muttered about possible causes for delay, like construction and a convention at a large hotel that could cause traffic issues. He wasn't talking to me or any of the other passengers, but I couldn't help paying attention. Hyperaware.

The driver was sandy-haired, although much of it was graying. He looked like a pleasant sort of guy, paying total attention to the job of driving and making good time despite the running commentary he was giving under his breath. With the kind of day I had been having, it was a relief not to have to worry about the people around me suddenly turning on me for no reason. The bus felt like a safe place for me to ride and think at the same time.

Lost in thought, I kept a corner of my awareness on my surroundings, just in case. The rest of my mind circled endlessly through a combination of dread, shock at my father's sudden supportiveness and concern, and keeping an eye out for suspicious people outside the bus windows whenever we slowed or stopped for passengers.

Before I realized it, we were there. This was the last place I would see in St. Louis, maybe for a very long time. I scanned the area for danger, though it was probably a waste of time and effort. I had no idea what I was looking for. I wouldn't recognize it if I saw it.

My heart started to race as the door opened and I got out with several other people, tossing the raincoat's hood over my head again to obscure my face. Wasting no time, I walked toward the entrance of the station. I'd never been here before, so I didn't really know what to expect.

What I did know was I needed to get the hell out of St. Louis. The sliding automatic doors opened, and I walked inside. The place was awful. Harsh overhead lighting illuminated a grimy, echoing space full of lost luggage and lost souls.

I would fit right in.

I found the ticket desk after only a couple of minutes of wandering around like a clueless idiot. Thankfully, nobody bothered me, or seemed to take any notice of me at all, really. There was a line, populated by a diverse collection of people ranging from wholesome-looking families with small children, to men I definitely wouldn't want to be caught alone with. When my turn came, I stumbled through the unfamiliar process, much to the obvious irritation of the guy behind the heavy glass.

Eventually, with his help, I figured out what bus line I needed, and shoved cash for a one-way trip through the little gap at the bottom of the window. Ticket in hand, I left the counter and wandered toward the sweltering passenger area to wait until it was time to board.

Two hours. I just had to keep my head down for two hours, and then I'd be out of the city. Out of the state, and—hopefully—out of Werther's reach.

I sat in a seat surrounded by sad and desperate people. To my left, a family of three. Mom, dad, and a baby who was squalling—*loudly*. Poor kid was probably hungry. Or maybe he was as grossed out by this place as I was. If so, I could hardly blame him. To my right, there was an old black man who looked like he'd stepped straight out of the roaring 'twenties. Suspenders, newsboy hat, vest, and high-waisted pants. He was quite dapper for such a stooped, wrinkled old guy, but his eyes looked lost and frightened.

I sat in the waiting area for more than ninety minutes, knee jiggling restlessly. My nervousness grew and grew, even though I couldn't pin down a reason for it. I didn't know if it was the people around me, or the memory of cops surrounding my house that did it, but I felt increasingly unsafe in this cramped row of plastic chairs. My heart started to pound in my chest as I thought about all the things that could happen between here and Chicago.

I cursed myself as the warning signs of a full-blown public panic attack clamored in my mind. *Jesus, no.* Please, *please*, not here, not now. But there was no stopping it. I knew that much from bitter experience. Gathering what little strength I had, I threw my backpack over my shoulder and practically fled to the women's restroom down the hall.

If I'd thought the waiting area was bad, the restroom was worse. It looked and smelled like it hadn't been cleaned in a month. Still, I preferred it to the open waiting area where anybody could see me losing my shit. I didn't feel safe here either, but this was the best I could manage right now.

Taking deep breaths, I huddled in the corner near the line of sinks and wiped away the tears that were falling again. What the fuck was I doing? I didn't have time to cry. I didn't have time to let my guard down like this.

It was no good, though. I slipped inside a stall and locked the door, then leaned against it. My heart pounded like it was going to explode any moment now. I couldn't catch my breath. Every time the restroom door banged open, I nearly jumped out of my skin. Still, I stayed hidden in the privacy of the stall… tried to relax.

Yeah, as if.

Time passed, and I knew I couldn't hide in here any longer or I'd miss my bus. I looked at my new phone. It was nearly time to board. I had to do this, I told myself as I left the restroom and headed out, rejoining the other passengers in the stifling waiting area. This was my best—and maybe my *only*—chance to get away.

I'd put my hair up in a high ponytail, hoping it would make it harder for anybody to recognize me, since it looked nothing like my hairstyle in the photo on my ID. Despite the heat and humidity inside the echoing building, I pulled my hood up as well. The dampness of my clothes from the earlier rain made me feel like steam was rising from my skin, sticky and unpleasant.

The sun was setting by the time the announcement for boarding rang out over the PA system. I shuffled along with the other lost souls as we were herded through a set of sliding glass doors toward the waiting buses.

Cops were everywhere, weaving through the crowd outside. There was one stationed on each side of the glass doors.

My heart stuttered and began to pound again, even harder this time. They couldn't possibly be here for me, could they? I mean—I hadn't done anything violent. Hell, I hadn't done anything, *period*—but surely they didn't make a habit of staking out area bus and train stations for someone with no criminal record who was wanted for small-scale embezzlement and tax fraud.

Did they?

It didn't matter. There was no real choice here. I could either go through those doors and try to get onto my bus, or I could back out and run. If I ran, then what? I'd already bought the ticket with cash. The bus was the only transportation to Chicago I could afford. And even if I had enough for a plane ticket out of Lambert Airport, security would be far tighter there than a bus station.

No, I had no choice. I had to try to brazen it out.

They probably didn't know what I looked like, and they didn't seem to be checking IDs. They were just wandering around, looking at people. I'd keep my head down and it would be fine.

I hoped.

Surrounded by the steady stream of people, I felt reasonably certain I could make it through without incident. I'd managed to sneak under the radar all day by blending in with the crowd and acting as normal as possible. As I reached the open doors, I walked through without slowing down, being sure not to look anybody in the eye.

Hood up. Eyes down.

My feet carried me along the cracked concrete walkway between lines of buses. My heart was still galloping, but hope grew in my chest as my flickering gaze landed on the overhead sign with the route number for the bus to Chicago. It was right there, less than fifty feet away. I hurried my pace, unable to stop myself.

A few short yards from salvation, a heavy hand closed on my upper arm, pulling me roughly to one side. My breath caught. *No, no, no…*

"Zorah Elaine Bright," said a gravelly voice. "Come with us, please."

Eleven

Two cops flanked me. They were large, towering over me, their blank expressions giving nothing away as they hustled me out of the flow of people. I was aware of nervous passengers shooting us side-long glances before scuttling off to their buses, faces caught between curiosity and relief that whatever was going on, it had nothing to do with them.

"Let go of me!" I grated as the police officers penned me against the grimy cinderblock wall of the building. I jerked against the bruising grip on my arm, to no avail—my eyes darting past them to the line of buses that had been my only hope of escape from this nightmare.

"I'm not the person you're looking for," I tried. "You're making a mistake. I've never heard of Zorah Bright." Even I could hear the pitiful quaver in my voice.

All the energy was draining out of me, fading into hopelessness as the steamy summer air tried to suffocate me. I felt like I was in real danger of passing out. My chest hurt, a stabbing pain behind my ribs.

"Turn around," one of the cops said in a flat voice, and then they were manhandling me again, pressing me face-first into the wall. Rough hands jerked my arms back and zip-tied my wrists behind me. The thin plastic was tight, cutting into my skin and blocking the circulation. Once I was restrained, they spun me around and marched me out of the transportation center.

"Am I under arrest? You're supposed to read me my rights!" I said, a bit desperately. As long as they acted like police were supposed to act, I could convince myself that things would eventually be okay. That I would eventually get a chance to prove my innocence, and all of this would go away, leaving only a bad memory.

The cop on my right glanced down at me with cold, emotionless eyes.

"You have no rights," he said, the words flat with finality.

They were still dragging me away from the crowd. Panic gripped me, and I started fighting. Screaming for someone to help. But the people shooting us uncomfortable glances only saw a crazed criminal in police custody. No one was going to leap forward and rescue me. Nobody realized that this was all wrong. Nobody knew that I was an innocent person being dragged off to god-knew-what fate.

Nobody cared.

Not even the cops. To them, it was clear I was just another lamb being hauled off to the slaughter. Why were they acting like this? Surely they realized that if they were caught treating an arrestee like this, there would be consequences?

"Why are you doing this? I'm a citizen! *I do have rights*!" I yelled as they dragged me further into the shadows of a deserted parking lot behind the station. It was almost dark now, only a streak of lighter gray through the heavy clouds above the western horizon remaining.

They didn't grace me with a reply, and my stomach sank. They weren't taking me out the front door to a waiting squad car. They were taking me out the back, to a dark, secluded place. This was bad... so very bad, and none of my struggles had any effect. None of my cries had attracted any attention, and I could see no sign of bystanders nearby. We were entering a poorly lit area. I thought the big building to our right must be the Civic Center, which put Triangle Park at my left. There were train tracks ahead of us—the white gravel of the verge a pale swath in the fading light—and a mostly empty parking lot around us.

My breathing grew erratic as we came to a halt and I saw three men in suits standing in front of a black Mercedes. The back of my neck prickled even before I registered that the center figure was Caspian Werther. He regarded me coolly. The two men with him had the same creepy, shiny air of otherworldliness. All three stared at me like they might stare at a mildly interesting bacterium on a microscope slide.

Werther's flat green eyes locked with mine, glowing faintly in the darkness. A slow smile crossed his lips then, and I swear every nerve in my body shivered into full alert.

The two men beside him wore suits almost identical to his. Both had dark sunglasses on despite the late hour, and stood with their hands clasped behind their backs in nearly identical poses. The one on the right broke formation to take off his glasses, revealing green eyes with the same dead expression as Werther's. He was *scary* disturbing, just like Caspian. The guy on Caspian's left did the same thing, his movements nearly identical, and every nerve in my body screamed at me to run.

I tried, setting my feet and fighting as hard as I could, but truth was, my body was spent. There wasn't much energy left in me.

I was so screwed.

My flesh crawled with the same instinctive aversion I'd felt in the restaurant… in the MMHA office… as though my skin was trying to peel away from my bones an inch at a time. Without a word, the cops shoved me, sending me crashing to the asphalt. Grit and bits of gravel bit into my knees as I landed with a cry of pain.

"No," I begged. "Take me to the police station! Don't leave me here! *Please*!" My plea fell on deaf ears. The two officers ignored me and simply walked away, not looking back.

I forced myself to look up at Werther, who was still staring down at me with that self-satisfied little smirk twisting his perfect mouth. *Judge. Jury. Executioner.*

One of the other suits stepped around me and grabbed my zip-tied arms. He used the grip to yank me to my feet, sending a wave of squirming repulsion racing across my body.

"Get your hands off me!" I growled, rage twisting and merging with my terror at the idea of any of these men touching me. My feet tangled together, exhaustion and weakness threatening to send me right back to the pavement. Only the punishing grip on my arms kept me upright.

"I'm impressed at your efficiency, Liege," said the one holding me. "You found this creature only a few days ago, and already, it is captured."

"*Creature*?" I hissed in outrage. "You're the ones acting like animals!"

"It put up something of a fight, I'll admit." Werther's voice was dismissive. Contemptuous. "But I've been at this for a very long time, guardsman. A part-bred mutt is no match for my network of watchers."

"This could be quite a coup for us," the other shiny guy said.

Werther made a considering noise. "The other side has been careless, but so have we. This creature has been wandering around the human realm for more than two decades, with no one the wiser. It should have been found and destroyed long ago."

I drew breath to say something—I didn't know what. This whole thing was so surreal that if it hadn't been for the raging pain and sickness in my body, I might have been able to convince myself it was all a bad dream.

The one that was holding me cut off any protest I might have made. "Let's get this thing locked up. I feel disgusted just touching it. As it is, I'm going to have to bathe."

"The feeling's mutual, asshole," I ground out. "If it bothers you so much, then get your fucking hands off me!"

Werther stepped closer and backhanded me across the face, the movement almost casual. My head snapped to one side, pain exploding in my cheek. I tasted blood where my teeth had cut into flesh.

"Get it into the vehicle," he said, making a production of removing a handkerchief from his pocket and using it to wipe his hand.

I knew one thing for certain. If I let them get me into that car, I was a goner. I would disappear and never be heard from again. As the one behind me shoved me toward the black Mercedes, I inhaled and sent a silent prayer to the powers that be. *Please, please give me enough strength to escape before these guys take me away to who-knows-what kind of fate.*

I gathered every ounce of energy—every trace of adrenaline remaining in my body—and made a last-ditch attempt to get free. Slamming sideways, I hip-checked the guy on my left, then lifted my foot and kicked the guy behind me as hard as I could in the kneecap.

My captor snarled, his grip never loosening. My heart sank. Clearly, I was too weak to pose even a mild threat to them at this point. Caspian Werther stepped in front of me and grabbed me by the chin, using the punishing grip to push me to my knees once more.

"If you know what's best for you, wretch, you'll stop fighting and accept your fate. You don't belong here." His voice sent shivers up my spine. "This is our realm. You are not welcome. Your very existence is a criminal abomination."

The last bit of hope drained from me. "I don't understand what's happening," I said, hating the defeated tone of my voice. "Why are you *doing* this?"

Werther made a dismissive sound. "Why does one swat a fly?" he asked.

The guy behind me grabbed the hood of my jacket and used it to pull me upright, then he and his buddy were hustling toward the car again. Toward a fate I could barely imagine.

The roar of a motorcycle engine cut across the background of city noises, growing louder by the second. It sounded like it was moving fast—far too fast for a parking lot. It also sounded like it was coming this way. I dragged my aching head up, trying to see where it was coming from. The glare of a single headlight half-blinded me.

"Is that—?" one of my captors began, only to be cut off by Werther.

"Move!" Werther snapped.

Before he could take his own advice, the engine roar grew deafening and a large, dark shape hurled past me, so close that the wind of its passage ruffled my hair. The motorcycle sideswiped Werther, sending him flying. His body hit the pavement hard and rolled.

Tires squealed on pavement as the motorcycle slewed to a stop, and a dark form stepped off of it. My heart leapt into my throat as a familiar figure with wind-whipped black hair and the ethereal face of a dark angel strode toward us, reaching over his shoulder to pull a sword—a fucking *sword*—from a sheath strapped to his back.

"*Rans*?" I cried, wondering if I'd just suffered a psychotic break and was hallucinating wholesale now.

He spared me only a brief glance, and when he did, his eyes were glowing… lit from within by the bluest of flames. Before I could do more than gasp, one of my captors was rushing him, an extendable truncheon snapping to full length in his hand.

"Get in the car, worm," hissed the one still holding me.

Only one option occurred to me, since I'd already had it proven that I didn't have the strength to fight them. I went absolutely limp, flopping to the ground like a sack of potatoes despite the agony in my shoulders as the man tried to keep me upright using my bound arms. I forced every muscle to go lax, making myself a dead weight.

Let the asshole try to get me in the damned car *now*.

Somewhere behind me, metal clashed and I heard the thump of flesh on flesh. I wanted desperately to crane around and look, but I didn't dare. Someone grunted, and the man trying to drag me the last few feet to the car hissed like an angry cat.

"*Get your hands off of her*," said a familiar British accent, from very close by.

I did crane around then, only to find Rans standing a step away from my captor, towering over me like an avenging angel in black leather, sword in hand.

"The Court will hear about this, parasite," growled the man holding me.

"I have no treaty with your Court. And I did warn you," Rans replied calmly. The sword flashed, and my captor screamed, staggering back to land with a thump against the black Mercedes as he clutched the stump of his right arm.

Something wet had flopped onto the pavement next to me. I very carefully didn't look, but that didn't stop my gorge from rising at the knowledge of what had just happened. Rans leaned in and grasped me by the upper arm, helping me stagger to my feet. He turned me to face away from him and murmured, "Hold still."

With the faint rasp of a blade against hard plastic, the zip tie binding my wrists snapped and fell away. Pain shot through my shoulders as I jerked my arms free of the unnatural position they'd been bound in.

"Time to leave," Rans said grimly, sheathing his sword and hustling me toward the bike.

I staggered, stumbling over my own feet, praying desperately that this unexpected final burst of adrenaline would hold long enough for me to cross the hundred or so feet separating us from the motorcycle. A firm grip kept me upright, and we were almost there when movement caught the corner of my eye.

"Werther!" I gasped, as the crumpled figure rose with impossible grace from where he'd been flung by a high-speed impact mere moments before.

Rans was already spinning me around, stepping sideways so that his body was between me and my miraculously recovered tormentor. I felt

Rans' body jolt with some kind of impact that drew a soft grunt from him. Before I could respond, we were moving again, and he was dragging me onto the bike behind him, gunning the engine.

I threw shaky arms around his body, scrambling for somewhere to put my feet. Werther was running... charging toward us, a vicious snarl twisting his too-perfect features. Panic clutched me as I stared at his fevered eyes. His outstretched hands. But then the bike peeled away, leaving me to cling to the solid form in front of me as Rans accelerated away from the scene of carnage in the parking lot.

My breath was coming in great, rasping sobs, and it felt like I couldn't get enough air. I leaned against the broad back in front of me, and my eyes caught and held on the flash of silver metal and the finely wrought wooden handle protruding obscenely from Rans' left shoulder.

It was a knife. Werther had thrown a knife at us as we'd been running for the bike, and Rans had purposely shielded me and taken the hit.

"Your shoulder!" I cried, the wind trying to whip the words away as soon as I uttered them.

"Least of our worries right now," Rans called back.

A flash of light in the motorbike's round little rearview mirror dragged my attention away from the horrible sight of the dagger protruding from Rans' flesh, and I twisted to look over my shoulder. Car headlights followed us, careening crazily as the black Mercedes jumped a curb to come after us in the most direct line possible.

"Hold on, luv," Rans warned. "Things are about to get interesting."

Twelve

My heart raced at about a million miles an hour as I maintained my death grip on Rans' waist. He wove the motorcycle expertly along the darkened streets of downtown St. Louis, not allowing the Merc to gain ground. I was hopelessly disoriented, but I had the vague idea that we were circling back, approaching the Civic Center again. Rans braked sharply and swerved into an alley with cars parked along one side.

There was no way the big Mercedes could follow us, even if Werther was willing to mow down smaller cars and crash through them like bowling pins. We emerged on a different road and Rans continued his unpredictable path through the city, speeding down one-way streets, barely clearing stopped cars as we wove between them at stoplights, repeatedly slipping past cars coming at right angles to us on cross-streets, with mere inches to spare. Horns blared in our wake, but it was inconceivable that Werther could track us this way in his massive, ungainly vehicle.

Rans slowed down for an almost sedate left turn, then twisted the throttle sharply and rocketed onto a freeway onramp, making my body slide back sharply before I caught myself. He merged with traffic and accelerated, speeding along, passing cars right and left—even moving all the way over to the center shoulder to swerve around a few.

The city flew by in a blur as we screamed along the expressway.

Rans zipped through a gap and sped down an off-ramp, exiting the freeway after what had probably been only two or three miles. I was clutching him so tightly that I didn't know if I'd be able to pull my fingers loose once we eventually stopped. My joints felt frozen in place. Petrified.

But… it appeared we had lost our tail.

Rans drove the bike through a narrow alley somewhere behind Enterprise Center. The bike jumped as we left the pavement and drove along the verge running beside the train tracks, gravel spitting from beneath the flying tires. I fretted silently about possible dead-ends or unexpected drop-offs, but there was method to Rans' madness. The next thing I knew, he'd followed a concrete culvert up a gentle slope and hopped onto the I-44, heading west.

My chest hurt. My head hurt. Everything hurt, but for that moment, I closed my eyes and rested my forehead on Rans' uninjured shoulder, just breathing. In, out. In, out. In, out as the wind whipped past us.

After a few minutes, I chanced raising my head and recognized where we were. This was the Central West End, site of many of the city's tourist attractions. Rans exited the interstate and drove sedately through traffic, heading toward a fashionable apartment building across from Forest Park, near the Zoo and Art Museum.

Rans turned into the driveway and headed down a ramp leading to a secure basement parking garage. He stopped to punch in a code at the gate, and the barrier lifted.

"Almost there, Zorah. Stay with me for a bit longer."

I wasn't sure what he meant by that. All I could do was hold on as the bike pulled into the underground parking area, my head swimming now that we were no longer speeding through the night. Finally, we came to a complete stop, the engine rumbling into silence. Rans braced the motorcycle upright and deployed the kickstand, letting out an audible breath.

We sat there quietly for a few seconds before he finally spoke.

"You can open your eyes now." A hint of dry amusement colored the words.

I scowled at his back. "Shut up. They're open."

God. I'd almost forgotten what that accent of his did to me. I knew I should still be terrified out of my mind. Yet something about being here alone in this anonymous basement garage with him settled my nerves. I felt surprisingly safe. Protected, for pretty much the first time in the last two days. It was a feeling I'd almost forgotten in that short space of time.

"Are they, now? I'm glad to hear it," he said. The amusement was still present, but tempered now with a hint of tightness around the edges. "In that case, you can do me a favor."

"Hmm?" I hummed, lost in my post-adrenaline haze.

"Be a dear and pull the knife out of my shoulder, would you? It's an awkward angle to get it myself."

That woke me up fast. I stiffened, straightening away from him despite the screaming protest from my body. "What? I... don't—"

"Grab the handle, and pull straight out. One smooth movement," he said patiently.

My stomach churned its displeasure at this idea, but what else was I supposed to do? I gingerly wrapped my fingers around the burnished wooden handle and tugged. The blade slid free with a terrible sucking sensation.

"Cheers," he said, as though he didn't have a bleeding hole in his shoulder. "You might as well hold onto it, now that you've got it. Silver's not much use against Golden Boy and his ilk, but that much of the stuff will be worth a few quid, at least."

I stared at the dagger stupidly. It was a work of art as much as a weapon. The rivulets of crimson that stained the blade resembled rich brushstrokes of paint on a master's canvas. My gut twisted. Something about the thing gave me a milder version of the feeling I got when I was around Werther.

"Is this seriously made of silver?" I asked in a faint voice.

He snorted. "Oh, yes. If it had been steel, my shoulder wouldn't feel like it's burning from the inside out."

"I don't like it," I said, still staring at the finely crafted knife.

"Really?" he replied. "That's rather interesting." He rummaged in a pocket and passed a clean handkerchief to me. "Believe me when I say I'm not too chuffed about it either... but hold onto it for me anyway."

It took me longer than it probably should've to understand that the handkerchief was so I could clean the blood off the blade. I tried to pretend I was wiping down a kitchen knife after slicing some kind of juicy red fruit. It didn't help. When I was done, I handed the stained square of cloth back to him awkwardly, not sure of the proper handkerchief protocol under these sorts of circumstances.

The freshly cleaned silver gleamed in the overhead lighting of the garage. My backpack was long gone—abandoned somewhere in the parking lot behind the bus station. I was afraid if I tried to put the dagger in my raincoat pocket, it would slice through the material and cut me. After a moment, I slipped it down the inside of my soft leather boot.

Rans had canted his body half-sideways on the seat of the motorcycle to watch me. I realized that sitting behind him like this, I had him hemmed in, so I stood up, bracing myself on unsteady knees. Once I was clear of the bike, he swung a leg over in a smooth, practiced movement and stood in front of me.

"All right there, luv?" he asked.

His eyes were such an unusual shade of blue. The inner fire from earlier was gone, but even now, I was in danger of getting lost in them.

"Yeah," I breathed. "What now?"

"We'll take the lift upstairs."

I did a quick English-to-American translation and realized he meant an elevator. I could see a set of stainless steel double doors in the corner, so I nodded.

"Okay," I said, and tried to take a step in that direction.

My vision tunneled in from the sides and the muscles in my legs turned to rubber. A strong arm caught me around the shoulders, keeping me from face-planting on the concrete floor.

"Hmm," Rans said. "That's what I was afraid of."

"I'm all right," I tried to protest, hearing how reedy my voice sounded. "M'okay."

"Yes, I can see that."

I breathed deeply, trying to push the gray fog from my vision. "Jus'… give me a minute…"

"I would, but I'm not sure a minute is going to help much." I was distantly aware as Rans pulled one of my arms over his shoulders and rearranged his grip around my waist. "Now, come along, tough girl. Let's get you someplace where you can sit down and rest while I get this mess sorted out."

I nodded rather than waste breath on words. Rans led me to the elevator and I focused on shuffling one heavy foot in front of the other. On some level, I became aware that I was leaning on a man with an untreated knife wound.

"Your shoulder," I slurred.

"One nice thing about black leather; it's brilliant for hiding bloodstains." The words were wry.

"But—" I protested.

"It's fine. It's already healing."

That… didn't seem right somehow, but I let it go. The elevator doors opened with a ding, then closed behind us a moment later, shutting out the view of the parking area full of expensive cars and one sleek black motorcycle. Rans pressed the button for the top floor, and entered another complicated code on the keypad next to it.

My heavy body grew heavier as we accelerated upward. He supported me easily, his grip never wavering. I knew I was plastering myself against him like a cheap whore, but I didn't have the strength to stand on my own.

And, if I were being honest, it felt… really good. *He* felt really good.

His leather jacket was cool against my feverish body. His arm around me was sure and strong. He smelled like some exotic blend of spices underlaid with musk. I wanted to nuzzle against the bare skin of his neck. I blinked rapidly, appalled with myself.

Even *now*, my mind was coming up with this kind of inappropriate shit? What the hell was wrong with me?

Fortunately for Rans' virtue and my sanity, the elevator came to a smooth stop and disgorged us into a posh entryway with a single white door across the way. He supported me over to it and mashed the button on a small intercom unit set in the wall.

"Guthrie, mate—you in there?" he asked. "Got a bit of a situation here."

A few moments passed while I tried to ignore the heat building beneath my skin and the pleasant tingles radiating outward from where his fingers splayed across my ribcage, supporting me. The click of a lock disengaging preceded the door swinging open to reveal a frowning black man with a vaguely familiar face.

Guthrie Leonides, my mind offered helpfully. Rans' friend from the restaurant the other day.

Guthrie's sad, dark eyes ran over us, the silence stretching for an awkward beat. I could only imagine what I must look like—half-dead and half-debauched as I hung all over Rans, staring back at Guthrie with my jaw slack.

"Do I want to know?" Guthrie asked eventually.

"Nope," Rans said briskly, popping the 'p.' "But if you ask nicely, I'll tell you anyway—*later*. For now, I need someplace to hide out and a couple of fake IDs. So, are you going to invite me in?"

My fractured attention swung to Rans' face, just in time to catch the faintly unhinged smile he threw his friend. My brain clicked a moment later, and I realized it was a joke. *Inviting the vampire in*.

Guthrie's answering expression was definitely nearer to the resigned end of the spectrum than the amused one. "Come on in, you undead English asshole. And hello again, Miss…?"

"Bright," I managed. "Call me Zorah."

Guthrie held the door open for us. Once Rans had maneuvered me through, he closed it and I heard the lock click into place. Again, I should probably have been terrified—alone in a locked apartment with two men I didn't know, so weak I could barely stand on my own. Instead, the sound of that lock engaging made the remaining tension

in my shoulders slide away into sweet, blissful relief.

Safe, my instincts insisted. *You're safe now.*

"I think I need to sit down," I said in a quaver-
ing voice.

"I think you need to sleep for the next day or
so," Rans shot back, eyeing me like he thought I
was about to pass out on him. It wasn't a completely irrational concern on his part.

Guthrie was also watching me with a worried
frown. "Take her to the guest room. Do I need to
get a doctor up here?"

"I'm not sure yet," Rans said. "Though it's
likely there's not much a human doctor could do
for her."

"Huh?" I blinked at him stupidly, trying to
keep up with the cryptic conversation while also
trying not to fall over. It was becoming surprisingly
difficult to juggle those two things.

"Right." Guthrie sounded grim. "I'm guessing
this falls under the 'No, Guthrie, you don't want to
know' part of things."

"I suspect so." Rans hitched my body a little
tighter against his. "Come on, tough girl. Let's go
find you a bed."

My belly tightened at the innocent words. God,
I was such a sick puppy.

Even as out of it as I was, I could tell that
Guthrie's penthouse apartment was amazing. I
wondered if he lived here alone. It certainly didn't
look like he had kids—everything was too perfect,
too untouched. I had a vague impression of subtle,

soothing colors and expensive artwork as we moved through living spaces and down hallways.

Then we were in a pristine, beautifully appointed bedroom that smelled like lavender and fresh cotton. Rans eased me down to sit on the edge of the queen-sized bed. The mattress was as soft as eiderdown beneath me. Part of me wanted to collapse backward into the bed's pillowy support and never move again, but another part clamored in protest when Rans' grip on me eased and pulled away completely.

Without even realizing I was doing it, I shot a hand out to twist in the cotton of his black t-shirt. He stayed bent over, watching my face, his glacier-blue eyes level with mine.

"How did you find me tonight?" I asked. "How could you possibly have known to come to the station at exactly that moment, so you could save me?"

His lips twitched into something that tried to be a smile, but his pale eyes were watching me, intent and piercing.

"Stalker, remember?" he said lightly.

I did remember. I remembered the way he'd showed up in my section at AJ's the day after he'd bitten me. I remembered him calling me an enigma, and the way he'd seemed to pull back from the conversation when I told him I had no idea what he was talking about.

"Get some rest, Zorah," he said in an even tone. "I need to figure out what to do about… all of this."

I stared into those depthless eyes, trying to see inside him.

"Okay," I said, feeling decidedly detached from reality at this point. "But... there's one thing, before you go..."

A small furrow formed between his dark brows. "Yes?"

"Just this." Without thinking, I used my grip on his shirt to pull him forward, closing the few inches between us until I could seal my lips over his.

Thirteen

Rans remained very still while I made a spirited attempt to perform a tonsillectomy on him using my tongue. Distantly, I knew that his lack of response should constitute a red flag of some sort, but all of my social skills were currently buried under an avalanche of want and need.

He'd ridden in on a black motorcycle and rescued me from a fate worse than death with a fucking *sword*. I needed him. I needed the press of lips against mine, the touch of skin on skin, the connection of bodies meeting. It was wrong, and humiliating, and pathetic, and right now I didn't care about any of that. I just cared about my tongue sliding against his.

Rans' hands hovered an inch above my shoulders for an endless moment before he grasped me gently and eased me back. I heard the pitiful noise of distress I made in response, and part of me hated it. That noise did not belong to the person I pictured when I pictured myself. Only... it did, didn't it? This was me, craning forward to try to reach the lips that remained just out of reach. This was me, panting shallow breaths as I tried to get back to the man who was pushing me away.

"This is going to be bloody complicated, I can tell already," Rans murmured, so low I could barely make it out. Then, louder, "*Zorah*. Look at me. Try to focus."

I *was* looking at him, though — watching those curved lips move as they caressed the words.

"Eyes *up*, soldier," he said, and I dragged my gaze from his lips to his eyes with difficulty. "That's better."

"What's wrong?" I asked. Why were we talking when I could be kissing him? Why did I feel like this?

"*What's wrong*? Quite a number of things, as it happens," he said. "Don't worry — I'm keeping a list for reference purposes. Right now, though, the item at the top… is *you*. I'm about to do something we both may regret. For what it's worth, though, you can always slap me afterward, when you're feeling better and you'll be able to put a bit of welly into it."

I stared at him, trying to get my neurons to connect. "Are you even speaking English right now?" I asked.

He stared back. "Am *I* speaking English? Of all the cheek! *Bloody Americans…* I don't know why I even bother."

"Yeah, me neither," I said, and pulled him toward me again.

This time, he didn't resist, cool lips slanting over mine as he pressed me back to lie on the decadent mattress. He followed me down, and every nerve in my body sang with the rightness of it. I writhed and moaned beneath the sweet slide of his tongue against mine.

The feel of a strong hand gliding over the contours of my body unknotted the painful tension in my muscles bit by bit. The ache of chronic illness morphed into a delicious ache of lust, and my trembling exhaustion eased into trembling anticipation. He was bracing himself above me on one bent arm as he kissed me, his elbow planted by my shoulder on the bed. His other hand slid over my belly, then lower. My legs fell open, inviting, and he cupped me through my jeans.

He didn't tease, thank god. His fingers rubbed between my legs with firm pressure. I was wet; I could feel the material of my panties sliding against my sex… feel the dampness where Rans pressed against me. The seam of the blue jeans offered an edge of stimulation against my clit, but it wasn't enough, it wasn't *enough*. I needed more, everything, all of it *right now*.

I scrabbled at the fastenings, tugging at the button and zipper and pushing the fabric down, down, panties and denim together. Rans broke the kiss and rested his forehead against mine.

"Bleeding hell, Zorah," he murmured into the air between us, the words tickling my swollen lips. But his fingers delved into the space I'd made for him.

I couldn't spread my legs with my jeans around my thighs, but that didn't stop me from making a noise I'd never made before in response to the first, perfect slide of his fingers. I wanted to strip us both naked and rub my body all over his like a cat, or like the vixen that was my namesake. I wanted to ride him… I wanted his mouth on me…

I wanted his body pounding into mine from behind.

I wanted so many things, but what I had was his fingers sliding into me while his thumb rubbed across my clit with every thrust. It was enough to bring me to the brink in minutes, and the nip of teeth across the sensitive skin at my throat where fangs had pierced me mere days ago was all it took to tip me over.

I jerked, keening, barely aware of the fact that I was in a complete stranger's apartment. I had no idea how thick the walls were. Or if Rans had closed the bedroom door behind us, for that matter. I didn't care about any of it. My body was singing, my earlier state of near collapse replaced now by the wash of pleasurable endorphins.

Rans eased me through the climax with lazy strokes of his fingers, and pressed a final close-mouthed kiss to my lips. It was so good… *so good*… but it wasn't all that I needed. His hand slid free of my body. I used my newfound energy to roll us, tumbling our bodies further onto the bed until he was the one lying on his back while I crouched between his legs.

Without a single thought in my head, I attacked the fastenings of his motorcycle leathers. He was still completely dressed, right down to his black leather coat. It splayed out beneath him like bat's wings, stark against the pale blue duvet.

"Zorah," he said, staring at me as my fingers tugged open the row of dark buttons along his fly. "You don't have to—"

I growled at him. Like, seriously *growled*, the way an animal would growl when something tried to get between it and its prize. His eyes flared for a moment with that blue light like the hottest part of a flame.

"Or maybe you do," he muttered. *"Buggering Christ."*

He was wearing black silk boxers beneath the leather, and I succumbed to the urge to rub my cheek against the sumptuous fabric. He drew in a startled breath and his cock twitched sharply. The heady smell of musk was more pronounced down here. My growl turned into a purr. I freed his thick length from the silk and leather, my mouth watering.

Rans was uncut—only the second uncircumcised man I'd ever been with. He was also hard and ready, a bead of pre-come gathering in the slit. It looked oddly coppery in the warm light of the bedroom, tempting me to taste. It *was* coppery, as though a hint of blood accented the usual bittersweet saltiness.

I probably should've had questions about that. I probably should've cared.

I didn't.

Rans hissed out a slow breath as I twisted my tongue around the glans. I teased, delving over and over into the slit. I wanted him to grab my hair, fuck my mouth, but his hands were fisted in the bedclothes at his hips. He held his body rigid, though he had rolled up to rest on his elbows so he could watch me. I liked that. My eyes met his, and they flared blue again as I slid my lips down his length. I felt his body tremble as he kept himself from thrusting up… felt it like it was coming from my own body, not his.

Like there was a connection between us, his sexual energy flowing into me—buoying me up.

I had intended to set up an easy rhythm, but each stroke of my lips felt so good. Each slow suck, so divine. I couldn't help speeding up, taking him deeper, hollowing my cheeks harder. His eyelids lowered to half-mast, blue eyes growing distant as though my lips were a drug, sapping his will.

I could sense his body tightening, preparing to give itself up to me, and a new surge of crackling energy flowed between us. I felt like a goddess. All-powerful. I took him nearly to the root, humming as hard flesh swelled at the back of my throat.

Rans shuddered and came, silently. I took it all… took him inside of me. I felt his essence flowing between us, leaving him and becoming mine. My throat vibrated in a low, female purr of satisfaction as I milked him of every last drop I could get. When he finally started to soften, I reluctantly pulled back.

God, I felt… that had been… *amazing*. Twenty minutes ago, I'd been afraid I might keel over. Now, I thought if I jumped off a roof, I would probably fly.

I sat up, gazing down at the powerful vampire I'd just taken apart with my mouth, and the first hint of trepidation began to creep back into my mind. Rans looked… pale. A bit dazed. He was watching me with an expression I couldn't quite parse.

I tried to reassemble the past couple of hours into a narrative that made sense. My brain felt like a computer rebooting after a catastrophic hard drive crash. An important fact presented itself, big red metaphorical arrows flashing.

"Oh my god," I said. "Rans, your shoulder! I'm so sorry... I don't know what I was thinking!"

Mortification flooded me, but Rans only flopped down to lie flat on his back and started tucking himself away. I realized that my jeans were still down around my hips and blushed bright red, scrambling off the bed so I could pull them up and fasten them. *Christ.* My panties were soaked—chilly and uncomfortable now against my skin.

"It's all right," Rans said slowly. "My shoulder's fine." He frowned. "Though admittedly, my scabbard is digging into my back like a sonovabitch right now." He shifted a bit, but made no move to do anything else about it. "Anyway, don't worry about it. You've had a rough day—I daresay you needed that."

I slapped a hand to my forehead, appalled at what I'd just done on so many levels I didn't know where to start. "That's no excuse," I argued. "My *god.* I can't believe I just did that!"

"Like I said. You *needed* it." He put a strange emphasis on the word. "Feeling better now, I'm guessing?"

"I'm fine," I said unthinkingly. "I... wait." I paused, listening to my body. Noticing, for the first time, the absence of all the things that had been clamoring in distress for days now. "I'm... *fine.*" My eyes flew to his. "*How can I be fine?*"

His blue gaze was still a little foggy. "Had a bit of a top-off, didn't you? The way I see it, it's the least I could do after the other day at your house. And it's not like it was completely one-sided, after all. I'll probably owe you another free slap for this, but you've got a mouth like nirvana, luv."

I gaped at him, still trying to process the last few minutes and failing miserably. Letting the nirvana comment pass, I focused on the part that seemed most important. "What do you mean, a top-off? Why do I suddenly *not* feel like two-week-old shit? And why do you look like you've been run over by a Mack truck, if it's not your shoulder?"

"You fed from me," Rans said, very slowly and distinctly, as though talking to a child.

"I sucked you off," I retorted, "and you fingered me. Last time I checked, a couple of mouthfuls of jizz doesn't *quite* meet the RDA for twenty-seven vitamins and minerals!"

"No, I expect not. That isn't what I'm referring to, though. It was my *animus*—my life force—that you fed on, not my bodily fluids." He huffed a breath of amusement. "Bodily fluids are my remit, not yours. Vampire, right?"

I shook my head back and forth, trying to make the world fit into these bizarre new parameters that seemed to have sprung up overnight. "Life force? What are you talking about? How can I feed from someone's 'life force' by fooling around with them for half an hour?"

A smile quirked one corner of his lips, but it was grim. "It's the demon in you, Zorah," he said.

"Feeding on sexual energy is what succubi *do*. Even, it appears, second-generation succubus-human hybrids."

Fourteen

My mouth opened, but since I had no idea what should come out of it, I closed it again. In fact, I did that twice more before finally settling on, "Don't be stupid."

Rans snorted. He dragged a hand over his face roughly, as though scrubbing away cobwebs, and rolled smoothly upright. He still looked wan, but his posture was straight and his eyes penetrating as he slid his black coat off and unstrapped the sword from his back.

"I told you the other day—you're an enigma, Zorah Bright," he said. "The blood I stole from you… it wasn't human blood. Or rather, it wasn't *completely* human."

My eyes strayed downward of their own volition, taking in the hard lines of an athlete's body visible under his black t-shirt. Tattoos wrapped around his right bicep and part of his forearm. The upper part of the black ink appeared abstract, but lower down, I could make out what looked like Chinese characters melded into the design.

I dragged my gaze back up to meet his.

"So," he continued, "Tell me about your parents."

"This is insane," I said.

He gave me a little eyebrow shrug as if to say, 'And your point is…?'

I frowned. "My dad's an accountant. My mom was a state representative."

"*Was*," he echoed. "How did she die?"

I didn't like the way old grief and fresh paranoia were scrabbling around the edges of my happy sex high. "A crazy guy shot her during a campaign rally while she was running for the US Senate. It'll be twenty years ago this July Fourth."

He nodded. "And the killer?"

"Hung himself in prison," I muttered.

"Anything unusual about your father?"

God, where to even start with that question…

"Not unless you count being kind of a passive-aggressive asshole as unusual. Although he earned some serious brownie points today." Damn. I needed to call him, too. Let him know what had happened. "He wired me money for a bus ticket. He was going to pick me up on the other end, too. Help me find some kind of legal help."

Rans nodded thoughtfully. "Just as well you didn't get that far."

"Why?" I asked, confused.

"Family members make excellent leverage," he said grimly, and a shiver of unease ran through me.

Had I put Dad in danger, too? How far did this thing reach? Whatever this *thing* was.

"I need to call him," I said.

Rans was still watching me closely with those piercing eyes. "I would strongly advise against that."

"But—" I began.

"Let's say someone is watching him," he interrupted. "If you fail to show up at the bus station and he doesn't know why, he's not immediately useful to them. But if he's in contact with you… if they intercept calls between you, then suddenly he's a rather attractive source of information."

A weight landed on my chest. "But… I bought a burner phone. Two, in fact. I've still got them." Fortunately, the phones had been in my pockets, not my lost backpack.

"And did he do the same?" Rans asked.

"No," I acknowledged with a sinking feeling. "I'd have no way of getting his new number, if he did. And I didn't contact him with either of the burner phones, so he won't have my new numbers either."

"Where is he?"

"Chicago," I said, still not totally sure why I was trusting this man with so much of myself.

He looked thoughtful. "All right. That's a fair distance away. Since they clearly know you weren't able to leave the city, with luck he'll be low on their priority list right now."

My head was spinning again. "You keep saying 'they.' Who are 'they'?"

"Your mate Caspian and his lot." Rans' voice dripped with disdain. "Since the war ended, they're the ones in charge."

I almost didn't want to ask, but… "The war?"

Rans must have seen how overwhelmed I was, because he shook his head. "Too much, too soon. Practical upshot—Golden Boy and his cronies aren't just going to let this go. They know who you are and, more importantly, they know *what* you are. They also know *where* you are—in a general sense, at least—though with any luck I can remedy that last part before it comes back to bite us in the arse."

I still wasn't ready to tackle the '*what* you are' part of things.

"Why do you care about any of this?" I asked instead. "Why are you going out of your way for me?"

He tilted his head, his expression thoughtful. "I have my reasons."

"Altruistic ones?" I asked tartly.

A brief smile twitched at his full lips. "Not originally. Though for what it's worth, you're growing on me. If nothing else, luv, you give *phenomenal* head."

He was trying to distract me from the real issues, I was pretty sure. And right now, I decided to let him do it. Too much had happened in too short a time. I needed a chance to sort everything out. If that was what he was offering me right now, I'd take it.

"Yeah? Well, you're no slouch in the foreplay department, either," I told him, my voice wry. "Or the ego-stroking department. Men mostly run for the hills after sleeping with me. I'd always sort of assumed that meant I was lousy at it."

Okay, I hadn't really intended for that last part to slip out. Possibly I was still more out of things than I realized.

Rans hitched a hip against the corner of the heavy wooden dresser across from the bed. "No. It means they sensed you drawing *animus* from them. Their instincts sensed danger, even though their rational minds couldn't understand it. So they ran."

I didn't want to think any more about this right now. I wanted to set it aside and… what? Come back to it later? What made me think it would be any easier to wrap my mind around this stuff a day from now… or a week, or a decade?

"I've always felt better when I was in a relationship," I said slowly. "*Physically* better, I mean."

He shrugged. "I don't doubt it. Starvation is a real bastard, no matter what species you are."

My stomach did a little flip of protest. "So you're saying I was… *feeding* on my boyfriends? What would have happened if they'd stayed? Would I have hurt them? *Killed* them?"

Part of my mind was still protesting this whole insane conversation. Another part was connecting the dots, thinking about how, the worse my body felt, the more insistent my sexual desire became. Chronic pain and fatigue should have had the opposite effect on my libido, but instead I turned into a walking nympho.

"It's hard to say," Rans said, and I had to cast my mind back to regain the thread of the conversation—my question about hurting my boyfriends. "They might have succumbed to you eventually. It's uncharted territory, really, since as far as I'm aware, a cambion has never successfully reproduced with a human before."

… and we were back to speaking separate languages again.

"Cambion?" I asked.

"The offspring of a human and a demon suc-cubus," Rans explained. "In this case, almost certainly your mother."

Damn it, now my head was starting to hurt again. "Wait… but… if I could possibly kill a guy by sleeping with him for an extended period, then what about my dad? He and Mom were married for years, and he's okay." I paused, and walked that last part back a bit. "Well… okay-*ish*, anyway."

"I've no idea," Rans said. "Maybe they were largely celibate, and she got her meals elsewhere."

I narrowed my eyes at him. "What the hell are you trying to imply?"

He blinked, and pushed upright from his cas-ual leaning stance against the dresser. "You asked. I'm just theorizing aloud. That's enough specula-tion for right now, though. You still need sleep, and I still need to figure out what the hell we're doing next." He sighed. "I was always rubbish at chess."

"That's reassuring," I told him, and was re-warded with that borderline scary flash of a smile I'd seen a couple of times before. It was a smile that said, *I might be a badass, sword-wielding supernatural creature, but that doesn't mean I still have all my mar-bles.*

"It keeps life interesting," he said. "Well… it keeps *undeath* interesting. You know what I mean."

"Actually, I only understand about one word in three that comes out of your mouth. And I'm not talking about the accent."

But at least you're pretty to look at, I didn't add.

"Oooh. *Touché*." He mimed a strike to the heart, and I was uncomfortably reminded of the gaping hole that had been blown through his chest the first time I'd seen him. Maybe something of it showed on my face, because he said, "Rest. No one's going to bother us here tonight, and you'll need your strength over the next few days. I'll bring you some food in a few hours."

"Food?" I asked sourly. "You're not just going to throw a rent-boy in here for me, so I can screw the life force out of him?"

His glacier eyes bored into me for a moment, though his voice when he answered was mild. "If I'm right about things, you're still three-quarters human—so you need to eat," he said, "and no, I'm not."

With that, he strode out of the bedroom with his leather coat slung over his arm and his scabbard clasped loosely in one hand. I noticed that he had not, in fact, closed the door after us when we came in here earlier.

Oops.

I flopped back onto the bed. My eyes caught on a rusty stain marring the sky blue of the duvet. It was blood. It must have come from Rans' shoulder when I pushed him onto his back, though I'd seen no evidence of the wound just now when he'd walked away.

This whole thing was nuts.

I scooted up until I was resting on the bed properly, my head on one of the fluffy pillows. He expected me to rest? He really *had* lost his marbles. I was still tired, sure—though not with the bone-deep, all-consuming exhaustion I'd been fighting earlier. But how could anyone be expected to sleep after the past few hours? Hell, the past few *days*? At least my body didn't hurt. For the first time in weeks, I just felt, well—*normal*.

Which… I guess irony could be pretty ironic sometimes, right? A vampire had just told me that I was part demon—right after I'd sucked his cock, mind you—and I felt *normal*. As pillow talk went, I felt like we both had some room for improvement.

I closed my eyes, telling myself I'd just enjoy my pain-free self on this comfortable mattress for a bit while I tried to sort everything out. I was out cold within moments.

———◆———

It was still dark outside the window when I blinked awake. The atmosphere of the room had that silent, middle of the night feeling to it. My body felt pleasantly rested, even if my brain was stuck in just-woke-up mode. Was it possible to be jet-lagged when you hadn't managed to leave the city you lived in?

I rolled out of bed, feeling vaguely bad about having slept on such nice linens with my boots on. At least I hadn't been the one to bleed on the comforter—though an argument could be made that I'd been the one to tackle Rans to the bed, resulting in *him* bleeding on the comforter.

I decided to go in search of the nearest bathroom. For one thing, I needed it. And for another, I might be able to get the bloodstain out with cold water. The hall outside was dark, lit only by the wedge of light cutting through the bedroom door.

All but one of the other doors in the corridor were closed. Fortunately, the open door was, in fact, the bathroom.

Like the rest of the place, it was tastefully decorated and posh as hell. White marble gleamed; black and white tile laid in a chessboard pattern led the eye to the massive claw-foot tub that dominated the airy space.

When I was done, I washed my hands and eyed the scalloped sink, trying to decide whether it would be worse getting caught trying to wash blood out of a stranger's duvet on the sly, or leaving said bloodstain for Guthrie to find later. Though I suspected it would actually be cleaning staff who found it, since I had a hard time picturing anyone who owned a place like this doing their own laundry.

After a few moments of internal debate, I chose the coward's option of leaving it for someone else to find. Outside, the sound of low voices reached me. I followed them, wandering through the darkened living area. Light spilled through an archway to my left. The voices grew clearer as I approached, and I paused a few steps away.

"Normally I wouldn't ask, but…" That, in Rans' English accent.

"Yes, you would." A sigh. "Go on, then. It's not like you can do any real damage to me, is it? Just try not to drain me dry. I've got a full day today, and you've already kept me up half the night."

"I'd apologize, but we both know I wouldn't mean it." A pause. "You're a good mate, Guthrie."

"Yup. That's me. And you owe me lunch next time you're in town."

A snort. "Apt, I suppose."

"Damn straight."

I cleared my throat and walked in as though I hadn't just been eavesdropping. Then I froze in place, caught by the tableau before me. Guthrie was seated on a barstool at the freestanding kitchen island with his back to me. He was wearing the same dove gray button-down I vaguely remembered him wearing when Rans had half-dragged me into the apartment, but it looked noticeably less crisp now than it had then. His left sleeve was rolled up to the elbow. Rans held his arm in one hand, and his lips were pressed to Guthrie's pulse point.

Glowing blue eyes pinned me as I crossed the threshold, gluing my feet to the floor, daring me to comment. Guthrie must have sensed my approach, because he glanced over his shoulder.

"Oh, perfect," he said. "An audience."

"S-sorry," I stuttered. "I didn't realize you were…" I floundered for an end to the sentence. "… doing that."

I still couldn't seem to peg Guthrie. There was an air about him—a sense of having been beaten down by some great weight until he'd just… given up. And yet, he lived in this stunning penthouse, obviously a successful businessman. A successful businessman who let fugitives crash in his home, no less, and was apparently good enough mates with a vampire to voluntarily submit to the low-rent Red Cross blood drive routine.

Rans lifted his head, still regarding me steadily. "You're staring," he said mildly.

I frowned. "So are you."

He blinked, and made a production of scoring the tip of his forefinger on a fang. A couple drops of blood fell onto Guthrie's wrist, and Rans released the light hold he'd maintained on the other man's arm. Guthrie flexed his fingers and grabbed a napkin from the pile in the center of the kitchen island, using it to wipe away the smear of red on his arm.

His dark eyes returned to me. "Hope you're not squeamish at the sight of blood," he said. "Otherwise, you might want to reconsider the company you're keeping these days."

Of course, I *was* squeamish at the sight of blood. Seeing your mother gunned down at a young age will do that to you.

I swallowed. "I guess it's cheaper than desensitization therapy."

A small flash of amusement shone through the blanket of sadness that seemed to muffle the light in Guthrie's eyes most of the time.

"I guess so," he allowed. "Though god knows what other kinds of therapy you'll need after spending any appreciable amount of time with this fucker."

"Charming," Rans said. "Do you kiss your business associates with that mouth?"

"Not generally," Guthrie replied, unperturbed. "Are you hungry, Miss Bright? If so, there's a plate made up in the fridge."

"Call me Zorah," I said. "And thanks. Yeah, I could definitely eat."

Guthrie waved me over to the stainless steel monstrosity of a refrigerator. "Help yourself. Ninety seconds in the microwave should do it."

I retrieved and heated the food, trying not to think too hard about the other meal that had just taken place in this room. The plate held scalloped potatoes, steamed vegetables with a light sauce, and what looked like… duck breast?

"Wow," I said, my stomach rumbling.

Guthrie grabbed some silverware out of a drawer, and set it next to the plate along with a napkin. I dug in.

"This is delicious," I told him after swallowing a bite of crispy duck skin flavored with orange. I pointed the tines of my fork at him, and then at Rans. "So, tell me how you two know each other. How did you meet?"

"Through a mutual acquaintance, I suppose you'd say," Guthrie replied. "Ransley here has a penchant for collecting human casualties of the war."

"Not just human ones," Rans said under his breath.

Guthrie shrugged acknowledgement. "True."

"The war," I echoed around a mouthful of potatoes. "You mean the one that supposedly put people like Caspian Werther in charge of things?"

Fifteen

"Yup," Guthrie said. "Not that the other side winning would have been all that much of an improvement."

And there it was… a trace of the kind of bitterness that belonged with such a beaten-down demeanor. Rans' face was still, giving nothing away, but I sensed a degree of tension from him that hadn't been there before.

Of course, that meant I had to pick at the scab a bit more. "Oh? Who's on the other side, then?"

"Demons," Guthrie said.

Okay, *that* was a bit awkward… assuming I was buying into the whole succubus thing, which I wasn't ready to commit to quite yet.

"Right," I said slowly. "Demons. And Werther and his bunch are… what? Angels? Because if so, angels suck and I was sold a lie when I was growing up."

"No. Your good friend Caspian is Fae," Rans said. "Unseelie Fae, to be specific. If angels still exist, they don't seem to have any interest in the mortal plane these days."

"Fae? As in… faeries? You realize how all this sounds, don't you?" I asked, my eyes moving between them. "All right, then. So… demons and faeries. Where do vampires come into all of this?"

Rans' tension returned. "I'm afraid I haven't got a clue, luv," he said, the careless tone at odds with the tight line of his shoulders.

I looked to Guthrie for some kind of explanation, but he shrugged. "Don't look at me. I'm just a lowly human. I get all this shit delivered secondhand." He eyed Rans. "If you're all set with the ID and credit card accounts, I'm turning in now. Some of us still have to be at work in the morning."

Rans gave a short nod. "Sure. I'll contact you next time I'm in the area, and you can collect on that lunch. I'll leave the bike here out of sight, if you don't mind."

"Yeah, whatever," Guthrie said.

"Thank you," I said as he rose and rolled his sleeve down. "For the food, and... well... *everything*."

He hooked half a smile in my direction, but it didn't make a dent on the sadness he carried around like an invisible weight. "Don't mention it," he said. "Take care of yourself, Zorah—I'm sorry you got caught up in this mess."

"Back at you," I said, though I still had no idea how Guthrie was involved in any of this, beyond being Rans' friend.

He disappeared through the archway and into the depths of the sprawling apartment, waving the words off carelessly as he went. I turned my attention back to the vampire across from me.

"Finish your duck," he said.

I nodded and got back to eating before the plate got cold again. "What did he mean about IDs and credit card accounts?" I asked.

"That's why we came here. Guthrie has an obscene amount of money, along with an obscene number of useful contacts." He quirked an eyebrow at me. "For the next however long, you are JoAnne Reynolds from Crystal City, Missouri, and I'm your husband, John."

A manila envelope slid across the table to me. I put down my knife and fork so I could open it, revealing a driver's license, a passport, and a credit card, all in the same fake name. The photo on the ID was of a light-skinned, mixed race woman who looked superficially similar to me.

I looked up, meeting blue eyes. "That accent of yours doesn't exactly say *southeast Missouri*, you know."

"Hush your mouth," he said, in a passable impression of an American Midwest drawl. "Not that it matters, really. Easy enough to make people forget to worry about it." The last was delivered in his more familiar English accent.

"I still don't understand why you're doing this," I said.

His eyes never wavered from mine. "You're a loose thread, Zorah Bright. I have a bad habit of pulling on those, just to see what happens. Does the thread come free, or does the entire jumper unravel?"

I stared right back. "And what happens to the thread afterward?"

"With luck, it has a better future than it would have had if Golden Boy and his cronies had taken a pair of scissors to it."

I considered that for a moment. "Fair point," I mumbled, remembering the moment of absolute clarity I'd experienced as Werther's goons had shoved me toward the open door of the black Mercedes.

A fate worse than death.

That blue gaze looked right through me, seeing too much. Then, it softened. "We have plane tickets to Atlantic City, where we'll stay with another friend of mine. He's better placed to determine our next move, and it's a more secure location than this one. The flight's in three hours."

"Thanks," I told him honestly. Had I said that to him yet? "I thought when I went to the bus station that I had this under some kind of control, but… I am so far out of my depth right now that I can't even see the fucking shore."

He sighed and broke that disconcertingly direct eye contact. "Welcome to my world," he said. "Don't mind the riptides."

How reassuring.

Still, he obviously had a better handle on this shit than I did. I returned to the last few bites of my gourmet late-night meal. When I was finished, I looked up at him again. "What time do we need to leave? And how can you be so sure of getting me through security? The cops at the bus station snagged me without even glancing at my ID. They recognized me on sight."

Rans leaned his elbows on the counter. "The flight's at five-thirty a.m. We should get out of here in the next hour or so. Time for either a shower or a nap, but probably not both."

"And security?" I pressed.

"It's likely that the police staking out the bus station were under direct Fae control. If anyone recognizes you at the airport, I'll be able to influence them and make them believe they were mistaken… assuming they're human."

"And if they're not human?" I asked, vaguely appalled that this was something I apparently had to worry about now.

Amusement touched his handsome features. "Then things will get a bit more frisky."

I shivered, remembering the carnage in the parking lot. "I doubt the TSA is going to let you stroll past with a giant freaking sword strapped to your back, you know."

He snorted. "It probably wouldn't be worth the hassle, true. Happily, swords are on the list of rather unlikely things that can be checked in luggage. Also, throwing stars, believe it or not. Americans, eh? Sometimes I really wonder about you lot."

"Seriously?" I asked. *Huh.* Maybe cosplayers had a political lobbying group I'd never heard about.

Rans shrugged without lifting his elbows from the counter he was leaning on. I slid off the bar stool and took my plate and silverware to the stainless steel double sink. After giving everything a quick wash and setting it in the basin to dry, I wiped down the counter and threw my napkin in the trash.

"I'll meet you back here in forty-five minutes," I said, feeling fatigue start to creep back in after my brief reprieve of not feeling like shit.

He nodded, and made no move to follow me as I left the kitchen, retracing my steps to the elegant bathroom. Forty-five minutes of sleep wouldn't make much of a dent, assuming I could get to sleep at all. I eyed the claw-foot tub and made an executive decision.

After locking the door behind me, I stripped down and used the sink and some hand soap to scrub my panties, which had borne the unfortunate brunt of my slutty horn-dog routine earlier. The towel bar was heated... of *course* it was. I laid the damp underwear over it, trying to get as much of the fabric in contact with the warm metal as I could. It would help dry them, at least a little.

There wasn't much to be done for the rest of my clothing—it was all I had to wear now. But, *hey*. Maybe JoAnne Reynolds hated doing laundry, okay? That would be my story, and I was sticking to it.

The tub was as luxuriously indulgent as it appeared, and I soaked in the hot water scented with lavender bath beads for as long as I dared before giving myself a quick scrub and rinsing off.

I arrived in the kitchen at three a.m. sharp, wearing panties that didn't stink of stale sex and were only slightly wet from being washed in a stranger's bathroom sink. Rans was waiting for me, having exchanged his bad-boy biker vibe for something more in line with what he'd worn to the restaurant the other day — casual, but still put to-gether.

"You keep spare clothes here?" I asked dryly. "What is this… Guthrie's Penthouse Apartment and Safehouse?"

"Be prepared, that's my motto," he said, un-perturbed.

I couldn't hold in a snort. "Don't try to tell me you were ever a boy scout. Because I won't believe you."

"I'm afraid my boyhood predates that particu-lar institution by a few hundred years," he replied easily. "But that doesn't mean I can't borrow their motto, now does it? Are you ready?"

I filed that throwaway line for future consid-eration and gestured at myself — slightly rumpled clothing, boots, and raincoat with fake ID and a couple of burner phones in the pockets. "What can I say? I like to travel light."

He spared me a quick smile. "Low mainte-nance, eh? Give me that dagger from yesterday. I'll box it up and put it in the checked luggage with the sword."

"What, no throwing stars?" I asked, feigning disappointment.

He huffed. "Sadly not."

I carefully drew the unfamiliar hard length from my boot and held it out. He gave the blade a sour look. "Hilt first, if you don't mind," he said.

I flushed and quickly turned the knife in my hand, pinching the silver blade between my thumb and forefinger. He took it by the wooden handle and placed it in a flat box padded with newspaper.

"So… silver, huh?" I asked. "I thought that was werewolves."

"No such thing as werewolves," he said. "And as metals go, it's not my favorite thing, no."

He stuffed the sealed box in a suitcase that was sitting in the corner. I eyed the large piece of luggage.

"So, if we're not taking the motorcycle…?" I trailed off.

"There's an Uber on its way," he informed me. "Come on—it'll be here in a few minutes."

I followed him out of the apartment after leaving a quick thank-you note scribbled on a napkin for Guthrie. We entered the elevator and headed down to street level rather than the underground parking garage.

"Why is Guthrie so sad all the time?" I asked. "I mean… he seems to have a pretty sweet life, except the part where vampires show up at his door in the middle of the night. But sadness hangs over him like a cloud."

"He made an unfortunate decision, and his wife died," Rans said without looking at me.

My face fell. "Oh," I said quietly, wondering if he'd driven drunk and gotten into a fatal accident or something. "I'm sorry to hear that."

He didn't volunteer anything else, and a few moments later we were leaving the lobby of the grand old building. A white SUV pulled up to the curb as though choreographed, and the passenger side window rolled down.

"John Reynolds?" the driver asked.

"That's right," Rans said without a hint of irony. The almost-convincing Midwest accent was back. If I didn't know what he was supposed to sound like, I'm sure I would have bought it completely. As it was, something about it grated.

There was no denying my tension at leaving the perceived safety of Guthrie's apartment, but the drive to Lambert was free of incidents. Rans printed out boarding passes at a kiosk and checked in the Suitcase of Pointy Doom. It felt odd not to have anything with me but the clothes on my back—no purse, no backpack, not even a proper wallet.

I was no fan of airports, mostly because airports implied planes. And I *really* wasn't a fan of planes. Not once they got off the ground, anyway. Though to be fair, it wasn't as though buses had proven to be a much safer option for me in the end.

The security line snaked around a long series of barriers, full of unhappy people with heavy carry-ons shuffling forward a few steps at a time. Children cried. Men in suits checked their watches. Considering it was currently around four a.m., I could only imagine how bad the line would be later in the day.

By the time we reached the TSA agent at her little podium, my back was starting to ache. I realized with a start that I was facing life without NSAIDS... my trusty bottle of ibuprofen consigned to whatever fate had befallen my backpack the previous night. Given that fact, I was doing surprisingly well. My almost giddy feeling of healthy normalcy was slowly fading, but I was still miles ahead of where I'd been over the past few weeks.

The TSA woman accepted my boarding pass and ID, scrutinizing it for a moment before looking closely at my face. I tried not to react—not to let my shoulders stiffen or my face betray worry.

"She's just got one of those faces," Rans said in a low, compelling voice. The American accent still sounded wrong, but something about his tone made gooseflesh prickle across my skin.

The TSA agent's eyes flew to his and caught fast. She blinked rapidly, a look of mild confusion sliding across her features before they smoothed. She returned to processing my ticket.

"You've got one of those faces," she said as she handed everything back to me.

I had to suppress a shiver. "Yeah, it's funny, isn't it?" I said in a determinedly light tone. "My husband tells people that all the time."

She smiled absently and I continued through the checkpoint to the conveyor belt. Boots off, raincoat and cell phones into a gray bin. Belatedly, it occurred to me that having two cheap cell phones with me might look suspicious. I should have stuck one of them in the suitcase. There was nothing for it, though, so I moved to the creepy full-body scanner thing and assumed the proper position, feeling both ridiculous and nervous as hell.

The operator completed the scan and waved me through, and I relaxed incrementally. With my boots back on and my raincoat slung over my arm, I waited for Rans to join me and we headed to the gate. After the line at the baggage check-in and the security line, there wasn't much of a wait before boarding. I spent it staring at the lights outside the floor-to-ceiling windows with unfocused eyes.

It wasn't until we were called to board that I realized where our seats were. "First class, *dear*?" I couldn't help asking. "Isn't that… kind of expensive?" I felt ridiculous in the spacious airline seat, sitting there with my rumpled clothes smelling faintly of yesterday's body odor.

Rans looked coolly amused. "Only the best for you, pet," he said, and damn it, I was growing to hate that fake accent more each time I heard it. "Window seat?"

My body went cold. "Er… no. I'm good with the aisle seat, thanks."

His blue gaze swept over me. "Fair enough."

When we were settled, I fiddled with a snag in the fabric of my jeans. The denim was dark enough to hide the stains where I'd been pushed to my knees in the wet parking lot, fortunately, but I was still going to have to figure out how to acquire some more clothes soon.

The cabin attendant was droning on about safety measures, and I did my best to tune out the discussion of water landings and flotation devices. When the plane rolled away from the gate umbilical with a lurch, my hands clamped around the armrests and my heart beat faster.

"All right over there?" Rans asked, and I swear if there'd been a hint of smugness or amusement in those words I would have smacked him there and then, powerful undead creature or no.

"Never better," I gritted out. "I live for days like this."

A pause, and I heard the sound of the window cover being pulled down, cutting off the view of the moving scenery outside. He was silent as the plane taxied along the maze of runways, stopping and starting while I tried to distract myself from what was about to happen.

Then it was time to take off. My eyes closed, and my fingernails dug furrows into the cushy upholstery of the first class seat as the engines powered up, the whine becoming a roar that propelled us down the runway and into the air with a sickening lurch.

Sixteen

God, I hated this part of flying so much. No one would ever be able to convince my mind that this was a real thing that humans could actually do with relative safety. There were dozens of us crammed into a metal tube with wings that had been painted to look like a giant Tylenol. Stick a few internal combustion engines on the wings—ones that would catch on fire if a sparrow got sucked into them—and… why were we doing this again?

My ears hurt, and I'd left my stomach floating somewhere along the Mississippi River, far below us. I jerked in surprise when cool skin touched mine, easing my right hand free of its death grip on the seat arm. My eyes flew open as Rans tangled our fingers together. He wasn't looking at me, and he didn't say a word.

The unexpectedness of the gesture jarred me out of my spiraling anxiety. I wasn't at all sure what to do with it, or even what to make of it, so I did nothing. Well… nothing except cling to that preternaturally strong grip. After a small eternity, the airplane leveled out. I let out a slow breath, hopeful that there wouldn't be too many course changes or bouts of turbulence, and that I'd be able to pretend for a while that we weren't hurtling through the sky at insane speeds.

"Drink?" Rans suggested dryly as I released my death grip.

I opened my eyes to find the attendant wheeling his drinks cart down the narrow aisle. "Tempting," I said, "but probably a bad idea."

The last thing I needed was another reason for my stomach to rebel if things got rough during the flight. I ordered spring water, while my seatmate waved off the attendant's polite, "And for you, sir?"

"Thought you enjoyed a good vintage of red," I muttered once the airline employee had moved on.

"I do," he said, clearly amused. "And I had a particularly fine one just a few hours ago."

There wasn't much to say to that, so I changed the subject. "Tell me more about where we're going. You said Atlantic City, but our tickets are for Philadelphia."

"There are no direct flights out of St. Louis. With layovers, it was faster to fly into the City of Brotherly Love and have our host send a car for us. It's only about sixty miles away."

I nodded. "And your friend? Tell me more about him. Is he a… person who also enjoys a good vintage of red?" I'd almost said *vampire*, but realized before it slipped out that talking about supernatural creatures in a public setting like this was maybe not the best plan. Oddly, that strange tension I'd noticed in Rans earlier returned at my words.

"Actually," he said mildly, "he's more of a whiskey drinker, when he drinks at all. I've known him for… a long time. I expect he'll have better insight into your situation than I do."

His voice was low enough to be relatively private, and he spoke in his natural accent. I pondered the rather vague words, trying to fit them against his obvious discomfort with my question. Unless I wanted to get drawn into a morass of double entendres relating to drinking blood, I wasn't likely to solve the little puzzle without more information.

Still, I filed away the fact that Rans didn't like being asked questions about other vampires, or about the supposed war that Caspian and his people had apparently won. The plane lurched a bit, and I caught my breath, steadying the plastic cup of water.

"This is a ridiculous way to travel," I said. "I mean… seriously. Who thought this was a good idea?"

He huffed a breath of silent amusement. "I don't know what you're complaining about, luv. I was once involved in a biplane crash. Very nasty. But you don't hear me whingeing about it, now do you?"

I glowered, but kept my voice low. "Unless it was a biplane stuffed full of garlic, I don't guess you had much to worry about, Mister Shotgun-Blast-Through-the-Chest."

"Nonsense," he retorted. "I imagine things could've been quite ugly if they hadn't put the fire out quickly enough. Whatever the case, this is still the safest form of travel. Crashes are rare, and I've already been in one, so I like to think I'm statistically crash-proof at this point."

"*Biplane*," I muttered. "You know, I can wake up from this dream anytime."

Another snort, this one less amused. "Best of luck with that. I've been trying for centuries; no joy so far."

I let the conversation fade into silence on that faintly bitter note. The flight was only two hours, and there was an entertainment screen built into the back of the seat in front of me. I poked through the menu until I found something mindless to watch, and pretended to focus on the screen. Rans lifted the window cover, revealing an expanse of Technicolor blue above a carpet of rolling white clouds.

My eyes kept straying sideways to his profile as he gazed absently out at the view beyond the cabin. Sharp planes, softened here and there by a serious furrow or a faint hint of crow's feet. Male beauty bordering on the unearthly, accentuated by those eyes that now seemed to reflect the blue of the sky he was gazing at.

Was I really ready to believe this madness I'd been thrust into? I was Alice—crashing through the looking glass, wondering what was real and what wasn't. But unless I'd truly gone as mad as a hatter, the fact remained that I'd seen this man with a hole blown through his chest. I'd seen him drink blood, and I'd seen him tear through three armed men with a sword. I'd pulled a silver knife out of his shoulder, and seen that same expanse of skin pale and unblemished an hour later.

I'd seen my life torn down and burned in the space of little more than a day. If there wasn't something more to the world... if there wasn't another reality hidden beneath the one I'd known, then I had nothing left.

After I'd white-knuckled my way through an uneventful landing, we disembarked into a larger and busier airport than the one we'd left behind in St. Louis. I had a flash of paranoia that we would exit the gate to find a group of too-perfect blonde men waiting to jump us and drag me away. In reality, no one paid us much mind.

It took a bit of time for the Suitcase of Stabbiness to catch up to us at the baggage claim. Eventually, it rolled around, showing no sign of having been a victim of any overzealous security screeners. Rans checked his phone and fired off a quick text, then gestured me to follow him toward one of the exits.

A black Escalade was waiting a short distance away, the windows tinted too heavily to catch any sort of glimpse of the interior. As we approached, though, the driver's door opened and the most striking man I'd ever seen in my life stepped out.

He was tall — easily six-foot-three. Ageless, in the way that distinguished men in their late forties sometimes are. His dark hair — cut short — was just beginning to recede at the temples, where streaks of silver stood out from the shiny black. His face had too much character to be called classically handsome, but it was sure as hell arresting.

Deep-set brown eyes took both of us in with a single quick sweep. He moved with a sort of spare grace—unhurried yet purposeful.

"Ransley," he greeted, surprising me by pulling my companion into a brief, almost paternal embrace. His voice was not so much deep as resonant. The single word sent a small shiver up my spine.

Rans returned the hug with evident sincerity, patting the newcomer on the back before they parted. "Nigellus," he said. "I didn't expect you to play chauffeur for us personally. We could have rented a car and saved you the drive."

"Nonsense, my dear boy," Nigellus said, as though offended by the very idea. "I would hardly have delayed the opportunity to meet you and your companion—not after getting such an intriguing message from you."

I hung back, trying to get a better read on this newcomer who gave off a decided whiff of danger despite his easy urbanity. The fact that I felt drawn to him on some unconscious level was a bit worrying. It wasn't sexual attraction—though his charisma was undeniable, he just didn't strike me that way. Honestly, the best way I could describe it was as the opposite of the effect Caspian Werther had on me.

With Golden Boy, as Rans insisted on calling him, I had the overwhelming urge to get out of Dodge as fast as humanly possible. With Nigellus, I was almost desperate to know more about him.

And that bothered me, because it implied that my reaction wasn't natural.

Whether it bothered me or not, though, it looked like I was going to have the opportunity to get to know him better, since he was to be our ride and, presumably, our host. That didn't stop my heart from giving a little nervous lurch as his attention fell on me.

"Ms. Bright," he said in that arresting voice. "A pleasure to meet you, even though the circumstances are somewhat regrettable."

"Nice to meet you, too, Mr. — ?" I trailed off, fishing.

A pleasant smile crossed his face. I could easily imagine a panther smiling like that at its prey. Or maybe a shark.

"Nigellus will suffice," he said. "Anything else would only be a pretense. Now, let's get out of this public setting, shall we?"

Rans stowed the Suitcase of Doom in the Escalade's spacious cargo area, and ushered me into the second row of leather-upholstered seats. It seemed rather ironic that I was now jetting across the country in first class seating, only to be whisked away from the airport in a vehicle that cost more than I'd made in the past three years combined. Hadn't I just lost everything yesterday?

I settled into the luxurious comfort of the oversized Cadillac, with Rans in the second-row seat across from me. The engine purred to life, low strains of some kind of soothing classical music playing through the sound system. Nigellus navigated skillfully through the airport congestion, and within minutes we were pulling onto a freeway heading east.

"Shall I stop somewhere for food?" Nigellus asked. "Or have you eaten?"

It took me a beat to realize I was the only one he could reasonably be addressing. I checked in with my stomach, but even though the East Coast was an hour ahead of St. Louis, it wasn't yet lunchtime. "I'm fine," I said. "Let's just get where we're going without attracting any more attention than necessary."

"A wise strategy," Nigellus replied. "You should probably be taking notes, Ransley."

Rans raised an eyebrow. "Oh? Are you implying something?"

"Only that a bit of discretion now and again can yield more successful results in the long term than picking the wrong fights at the wrong times." Nigellus' dark eyes glanced at us through the rearview mirror.

"You've been listening to gossip." Rans' voice was flat.

"I always listen to gossip. How else am I to keep a finger on the pulse of current events? Really, though… slicing off the arm of an Unseelie guard in the middle of a populated human city?"

I remembered the wet slap of my captor's dismembered limb against the pavement, and was glad I'd declined the offer of a meal.

"That was my fault," I blurted. "Or, rather, it was because of me. He was trying to save me from being kidnapped."

"I am aware," Nigellus said. "And while that was clearly a worthy goal, it was also a politically sensitive one that might have been handled with a bit more finesse and a bit less wholesale amputation."

"I'll keep that in mind the next time Caspian and his goons get their hands on living, breathing proof of a treaty violation," Rans said.

"Your point is taken," Nigellus allowed.

I sat forward in my seat, grasping the backrest in front of me so I could get a better look at Nigellus' profile, as I asked the first of many questions I wanted answered.

"Tell me about this war. Rans said you know about this stuff, right? Because I've been dumped headfirst into the deep end of a world I knew nothing about until a couple of days ago."

Dark eyes caught and held mine through the reflective medium of the rearview mirror. Again, I felt the odd sensation of kinship, of fascination. I bit the inside of my cheek hard.

"You're demonkin," he said, "though the trace is fainter than I'm used to sensing. Your existence poses something of a conundrum for those of us in the nonhuman world, Ms. Bright."

"Call me Zorah," I shot back, "and answer the question, please."

Nigellus cocked an eyebrow and returned his eyes to the road. "As you wish. Before you can understand the war, you must understand that there are different realms occupying the same space as the Earth you know. Each is populated by a different… species, I suppose you'd say."

"Like… alternate dimensions?" I asked, digging deep into my brief flirtation with being a sci-fi nerd girl as a teenager.

"If you like," he agreed. "There is overlap between the realms. Weak spots in the fabric, where things can pass through. The human realm had the unfortunate luck to be a fertile, productive land with many things of value to those in the other realms."

"Go on," I prompted, trying to keep half an eye on Rans while also focusing on the answers I was finally getting. My vampire companion seemed to have gone very silent all of the sudden.

"As often happens, greed overcame the better natures of those in Hell, and in the Fae realm of Dhuinne," Nigellus continued. "Both the Demons and the Fae began to infiltrate the human realm in search of wealth and power."

"Wait," I said. "You're saying Hell is a real place?"

Jesus tap-dancing Christ. My fundamentalist grandmother would be having a field day with this if she were still alive.

"Indeed. Not to disappoint you, but it's relatively free of fire and brimstone—though it is a rather barren place. I fear demonkind was on the losing side of the propaganda war that the Fae waged on Earth, as well as the actual war."

I took a moment to wrap my brain around that. "What… so faeries started a smear campaign against demons to make humans hate them? That's…" *Crazy? Ridiculous? Unbelievable?* "… pretty smart, actually," I finished.

"Smart, and quite effective, as it turned out," Nigellus agreed. "The earthly realm was caught between two forces made up of individuals both good and bad—inasmuch as such a moral framework has relevance outside of human society. But over the millennia, humans learned to fear and hate demons. Not that the Fae didn't command fear as well, but they also commanded a kind of fascination."

"But no one much believes in faeries anymore," I pointed out. "While a lot of people still believe in demons." With a shiver, I remembered the description of the message scrawled on a jail cell wall in blood, the night my mother's assassin had hung himself.

Kill the demons.

It was Rans who spoke. "Since the end of the war, the Fae have been going to great lengths to erase themselves from human consciousness. It's easier to infiltrate than to conquer."

"Certainly, it's easier to rule from within than without," Nigellus agreed.

"When did all of this happen?" I asked. "I mean, was the war a recent thing, or…?"

"Oh, yes—quite recent," Nigellus said. "There was no official declaration of hostilities, but the conflict began around the fall of the Roman Empire, and the treaty ending it was struck in the late eighteenth century."

I stared at his profile for a moment, in case he was joking. He didn't seem to be.

"The late eighteenth century," I echoed. "Okay, so… talk to me about this treaty. I guess it says the faeries can fuck over humans to their hearts' content? That's totally awesome."

Nigellus paused for a moment as though choosing his words. "The end of the war was less of a clean victory and more of a... messy draw, shall we say. In addition to gaining control over Earth's resources, demonkind had also sought to gain control over the Fae themselves. Obviously, it didn't work out that way."

"So I gather."

"Under the treaty, the Fae retain their independence with a single exception—they must pay a tithe to Hell. In exchange, demonkind agreed not to interfere in the human world anymore... all of which makes your existence a rather interesting conundrum, as I said before."

I was still struggling to keep up. "In what way?"

"You're part succubus," Rans said, rejoining the conversation even though his shoulders were still tense. "That was considerable interference on someone's part."

I blinked. "And all of this is my fault *how*, exactly? Assuming it's even true in the first place... and I haven't conceded that point yet."

"Fault isn't precisely the point," Nigellus said.

"So I'm... what? Some kind of political football?" I pressed.

"An *inconvenient* political football, yes." Nigellus might as well have been discussing the weather, for all the emotion in his tone.

Again, I worried why I was so drawn to him when by every objective measure, he came across as one seriously scary mofo. Though I suppose he deserved points for taking us in, not to mention driving sixty miles on short notice to pick us up from the airport.

He glanced in the mirror, but this time his gaze landed on Rans. "How did you discover her in the first place? The signs are hardly obvious."

I let my gaze fall heavily on Rans, as well, wondering if he'd admit to committing wholesale shed destruction and unprovoked neck molestation.

He looked irritated. "*Hardly obvious*? We'll have to agree to disagree on that, I think. As it happens, I fetched up in her garden shed to rest for a few minutes after a Fae agent blew a hole through my chest with a shotgun. I drank from her to replenish myself, thinking she was human. Her blood has... some rather distinctive properties."

Nigellus snorted. "Oh, dear. That would explain it, I suppose. For an undead erection lasting more than four hours...?"

"*Excuse* me?" I squeaked, trying not to blush crimson. "Holy shit, was *that* what you meant by the quip about my blood being 'stimulating'?"

Apparently, not even vampires could burn someone to ashes with the power of their gaze. Otherwise, Nigellus would presumably have gone up in a puff of smoke under the dark look Rans was leveling at the back of his head.

"Yes. It was," he said, biting off the words, one by one. "Nigellus, don't be crass."

"You're absolutely right, of course," Nigellus said diplomatically. "Forgive me, my dear. I forget that all this is new to you."

"It's going to continue to be new to me until I get the answers I need," I snapped. "So, give me some. I assume you're a vampire as well?" It was a guess, but it seemed a logical one based on Nigellus' darkly striking looks and the aura of otherworldly danger that seemed to lurk beneath the cultured exterior.

"No," Nigellus said, as though I'd surprised him. "What would give you that idea?"

He sounded genuinely taken aback.

Beside me, Rans shifted. He was looking out the window, and didn't move his gaze from the scenery outside as he spoke.

"There are no other vampires," he said quietly.

Seventeen

"*There are no other vampires.*"

Rans' voice had been so low as to be nearly inaudible.

"What… *none*?" I frowned, having difficulty taking that on board. "Why not? What happened?"

He waved a careless hand toward Nigellus in the driver's seat. "You'll need to ask someone else that question. I have no memories at all of either the war, or its immediate aftermath."

"All of the other vampires were killed in the fighting," Nigellus explained. "They were allied with my people during the last few centuries of the conflict."

I mulled that over for a few moments. "So… that makes you a demon, Nigellus?"

"For my sins," he said lightly.

Another short pause. "I thought you weren't allowed to interfere in the human realm," I pointed out. "Aren't you doing exactly that right now?"

"Neither of you are human," Nigellus replied smoothly.

Rans gave a derisive snort, though he still didn't look away from the window.

"Technicalities have value," Nigellus insisted. "To answer your question more fully, Zorah, there are unwritten rules. Places where the Fae don't generally care to go, and where Demons still maintain a low-key presence."

"Places like Atlantic City?" I hazarded.

"Atlantic City... Monte Carlo... Las Vegas... New Orleans. There are a few others," he agreed. "Some places are more conducive to Fae magic than others, and as a species they're not fond of either technology or rampant vice."

"Whereas demons are all about rampant vice?"

"Demons are morally adaptable, within limits," he allowed. "Morally, and... otherwise. Though, even given that adaptability, I must say I'm surprised that you've managed to pass as human for... what? Two decades or more on your own? That's rather extraordinary."

I thought of my chronic health problems, my relationship issues with family and lovers alike, my nagging unhappiness, and my inability to quite fit in anywhere. A bitter smile pulled at my lips.

"What can I say?" I quipped. "I guess it's a gift."

Conversation trailed off after that. Both Rans and I were surrounded by our own dark clouds of discontent, and Nigellus seemed content to let us stew. What I had just been told was fantastical. Ridiculous. So why did it also feel like the missing jigsaw puzzle piece that, when slotted into place, would help my life make sense?

After all, I'd been so convinced that there was more to the world than what we were told. Now the explanation was being handed to me on a platter, garnished with mystery, uncertainty, and danger. Was knowing the truth better than remaining ignorant, even if it meant my life was in danger?

I wasn't sure.

A little over an hour later, we pulled up to what could, without too much of a stretch, be called a mansion. Nigellus turned out to be a consummate host, showing us to our respective guest rooms before giving us an abbreviated tour of the house and grounds. For some reason, it surprised me that the place was done up in cool pastel shades, the rooms light and airy, the decor inviting.

It did *not* surprise me that Nigellus had a butler. A freaking *butler*, like Alfred from the Batman movies. Nigellus introduced him as Edward, and it was obvious that he, too, knew Rans from long acquaintance.

"How lovely to see you again, sir," the elderly gentleman enthused, shaking Rans' hand in both of his wrinkled ones. "Allow me to get you and your lady friend a drink." His bright eyes slid to me. "And perhaps a light brunch after your journey?"

I declined the food but accepted a glass of iced lemonade, sipping it in the kitchen while Rans nursed a glass of rosé wine. Nigellus excused himself to deal with some business, whatever that meant. Edward puttered around, prepping food for the evening meal. The old man was impossible not to like, and I wondered how on earth he'd ended up working as household staff for a demon.

Somehow, it seemed impolite to ask.

"You'll need to acquire some basics," he told me as he chopped vegetables. "Clothing, toiletries. Would you like me to have those things delivered?"

To say I wasn't used to having a butler on call was putting it mildly. "I can't ask you to do that, Edward," I said. "I've got a bit of cash on me. I can pick up the essentials if there's a Wal-Mart or something nearby."

Rans made a disgusted noise. "Nonsense. We're practically on top of the boardwalk here. I'll take you out shopping. You can use Guthrie's card—his accountants won't even notice such a negligible amount."

For a moment, I was caught between paranoia at the idea of going out in public like a normal person who wasn't being hunted by pissed-off faeries, and irritation at myself for allowing that paranoia to control my actions. I didn't think Rans would have suggested it if it wasn't safe, and it seemed wrong somehow not to take advantage of an opportunity to see someplace I'd never been before. It was a beautiful day, and a beautiful city, and... well... *screw* the damned faeries.

"I'm game," I said. "Let's do it."

Which is how I found myself browsing adorable vintage clothing stores and old-timey drugstores on the Atlantic City boardwalk with a vampire wearing Ray-Bans; dragging an ever-growing number of bags around while ignoring my increasing fatigue and achiness. We stopped at a little cafe to rest for a bit, sitting at a wrought iron table shaded by trees while I wolfed down an

Asian-inspired salad with chicken and orange sections.

"So, tell me more about yourself," I urged around a mouthful of lettuce drenched in sesame-ginger dressing. "You know way too much about me, and I know next to nothing about you. You're English, obviously. Where were you born?"

He was watching me tear through the salad with evident fascination, but I refused to let it bother me. Now, he settled back in the chair, determinedly casual. Other voices buzzed around us, combining with the sound of wind rustling through leaves to ensure that our conversation would be private as long as we spoke quietly.

"As it happens, I was born in Yorkshire," he said. I nodded, still chewing. "… in thirteen twenty-one," he finished.

I choked on the bite of salad.

"Thirteen… twenty-one?" I rasped once I'd dislodged the lettuce from my trachea. "As in, thirteen twenty-one *A.D.?*"

"You asked," he said mildly.

And I had. It wasn't like he hadn't been dropping hints pretty much since I'd met him that he was old. In fact, I wasn't certain why hearing him rattle off an actual year should make such a difference to me. It did, though. If he was to be believed—and almost despite myself, I *did* believe him—then he'd been born in the freaking *Middle Ages*.

"What was it like?" I couldn't help asking.

Both eyebrows lifted behind the reflective black of the sunglasses, as though I'd surprised him.

"It was harder in some ways, and easier in others," he said after a beat. "I was… the oldest son of Thomas and Lisabeth Thorpe. I had two younger brothers and three sisters. The family ran an iron smelting operation, processing ore from the northern mines. It was sweaty, backbreaking work, but it was honest, and at the end of the day you had something to show for it. We never went hungry."

"I can't even imagine how different things must have been back then," I said softly.

He gave a barely perceptible half-shrug. "I was two years shy of my thirtieth birthday when the Black Death came to York. We had no conception of disease organisms and the way contagion worked… it all seemed so terrifyingly random. Families turned on other families, accusing them of witchcraft, or of drawing the plague to the city by not being devout enough."

"That's terrible," I breathed.

"Human nature has always been to lash out when danger threatens," he said. "When my youngest sister fell ill, my brothers urged my father to turn her out of the house, but my mother wouldn't hear of it. The rest of us got sick one by one. Eight days later, I was the only member of my family left alive—too weak to bury the bodies, or even to rise from my pallet so I could feed myself."

I found myself holding my breath, caught up in the story. Aching for the man seated across from me.

"Someone barred the door of our house from the outside, not that I had the strength to go anywhere in the first place," he continued. "I remember being afraid that the other villagers would set fire to the place with me inside. That, and the agony of thirst, like my throat was burning up. I could see a jug across the room. I was sure it had ale in it, but I couldn't get to it and there was no one to bring it to me."

A lump rose in my throat as I pictured it.

"I'm certain I would have perished by the following morning," he said. "The plague is a ravenous and impatient killer, for humans—or at least, it was back then. But that night, someone unbarred the door and entered the house. It was pitch-black, or else I'd already gone blind. I was barely aware of fangs sliding into my throat, drinking my tainted blood until I slipped into death's cool embrace. I woke some time later, frantic, with someone else's blood in my mouth... running down my chin. My heart wasn't beating. The lack of a pulse nearly drove me mad before I figured out what had changed."

My heart was beating fast enough for both of us by that point. "You were... turned by another vampire?"

"Apparently, the foolish bastard thought he was doing me a favor," Rans said lightly. "He buggered off as soon as the job was done."

My jaw dropped. "He just *left you there*? With no idea what had happened to you?"

"More or less."

"What a complete asshole!" I said, loud enough to draw a couple of looks from the tables around us. I sank back into my chair, blood rising to my cheeks.

Rans' expression turned wry. "Well, if it's any consolation, he's dead now, so…"

I could hear bitterness behind the gallows humor, but before I could respond, he changed the subject.

"Enough about me. I'm not the enigma," he said. "Tell me more about your family. Your mother was a politician and your father is an accountant. What do you know about your grandparents?"

I took a moment to change mental gears. "Uh… my dad was never close with his parents. I didn't have much contact with them. His father is dead, and as far as I know, his mother is still alive and living somewhere in Florida."

He nodded. "And on your mother's side?"

"Bit more scandal on that side," I told him. "My maternal grandfather was only with my grandma for a short time. He disappeared soon after she gave birth to Mom."

"Anything else unusual on that side of the family history?" he prodded.

"A couple of things, yeah." I sighed. "So… I've got photos of Grandpa and Grandma, right? They're both Caucasian. But Mom had the same kinky hair as me, and her skin was even darker than mine. Mom and Grandma always laughed it off, saying things like, 'Oh, genetics can be unpredictable sometimes.' But it seems way more likely to me that Grams had an affair with a black guy, and that's why my grandfather left her."

Rans tilted his head, regarding me closely. "Not necessarily. Did you ever talk to her about it?"

"Not really," I said. "She committed suicide when I was thirteen. She was always a bit unstable, but she got way worse after my mom was killed. One night she took a whole bottle of pain pills, and no one found her until the following day."

God, when I stopped to think about it, my family was a real clusterfuck. I was glad when Rans didn't offer any bland expression of sympathy. I'd always hated that kind of insincere shit.

Instead, he rested his elbows on the table and laced his fingers together, looking thoughtful. "It seems likely that your maternal grandfather was the demon. Unless you happen to be a student of the occult, you probably wouldn't know that demons can't reproduce. There are a set number of them. They are functionally immortal. But they can't sire children, or birth them."

Okay… now I was confused. "Then why do you keep saying I'm part demon?"

"Let me finish. There are different kinds of demons. Incubi and succubi feed off sexual energy. They also have the ability to hijack the human reproductive cycle, though the treaty with the Fae expressly forbids such a thing."

"Hijack it how?" I asked.

"Incubi and succubi can change sex at will. A succubus—the female form—can seduce a male human and obtain his genetic material when he ejaculates. Then the demon changes sex and seduces a female human as an incubus. If he's quick enough, he can use the stolen human sperm to impregnate the woman. But the process means that the resulting baby has demon characteristics, thanks to the magical changes to the stolen DNA."

"Okay. That's… quite a story," I said.

"Practical upshot—if your incubus grandfather seduced a black man to get the genetic material he used to impregnate your grandmother, it would explain your mother's interracial physical characteristics."

"… oh," I managed, as the point slid home.

"Of course," he continued, "that still doesn't explain how your mother had *you*, but perhaps that's a question for another day. If you're finished, we should probably head back." He gestured to the remains of my salad with his chin.

"Yeah," I said absently, new information whirling in my head. "Sure thing."

Eighteen

When we returned to the house at around two p.m., we found Nigellus seated in a chair in the living room, a heavy hardbound book resting in his lap. He looked up as we entered, a furrow forming between his brows as he examined me.

"You look fatigued, Zorah," he said. "Would you care to rest for a few hours before dinner? We will be dining at seven."

I froze, not used to people noticing when I was struggling with my physical limitations. It was true—I'd been feeling progressively worse over the last few hours despite the break for a late lunch at the cafe. Yet, compared to how bad things had gotten before, it was nothing. I'd mostly been ignoring the nagging pain and heaviness in my body, though I'd surreptitiously popped a couple of ibuprofen from the bottle I'd picked up at the drugstore.

"You should have said something," Rans murmured.

Why? the smartass in me wanted to ask. *Would you have suggested a quickie under the boardwalk if I had?*

"It wasn't a problem," I said instead. "I'm used to pulling waitressing shifts while feeling far worse than this."

"Nonetheless," Nigellus said smoothly, "you should feel free to relax for the rest of the afternoon. I'm afraid I must pull Rans away from you for a bit. I need to speak privately with him about an unrelated matter."

Maybe I was more tired than I thought, because I probably should have been more curious about that rather cryptic statement. As it was, I said, "Sure. I'll just hang out in my room for a while. Maybe take a nap. I'll… uh… see you both at dinner, I guess."

"Until then," Nigellus said.

He rose, ushering Rans toward the archway leading to the kitchen. Rans gave me a lingering, pensive look before exiting the room, and a small shiver prickled its way up my spine.

I shook off the odd moment. The pile of shopping bags was still sitting in the entryway. I felt like a pack mule carrying all of them at once, but I had the distinct impression that if I left them, Edward would end up lugging them upstairs on his eighty-year-old knees without being asked.

The guest bedroom was as cheerful and airy as the rest of the house. I dumped the bags on the green-striped loveseat in the corner and started rummaging. I found a pair of nail scissors in the bathroom and used it to cut the tags off the silky black knee-length nightgown I'd bought.

Finally being able to change out of the clothes I'd been wearing for more than two days felt wonderful. I considered showering, but frankly the bed held more appeal. Light streamed through the gauzy curtains covering the window. I grabbed the copy of *The Return of Sherlock Holmes* that I'd picked up for ninety-nine cents at a used bookstore and curled up on the emerald comforter to rest and read for a bit.

My fingers had lingered on a dog-eared paperback copy of Bram Stoker's *Dracula* at the bookstore, but it had seemed a bit too... on the nose, I guess you'd say. Reading about Sherlock Holmes' dramatic return from the dead was a lot less fraught. I made it as far as the capture of Colonel Sebastian Moran in *The Empty House* before my eyes slipped shut, the old book dropping onto my chest, forgotten.

———◆———

The sound of the door opening woke me. The light slanting through the window was at a slightly lower angle, but it was not yet evening. It hadn't occurred to me to lock the door—I felt safe enough here, and it seemed kind of a silly thing for me to do when I was a guest in someone's house.

That 'someone' is supposedly a demon, my inner cynic pointed out.

I blinked rapidly and rolled into a sitting position, just in time to see Rans catch himself against the doorframe with one hand. Blue eyes fell on me, but there was a dazed look behind them that I hadn't seen there before. He froze, as though he hadn't expected me to be there.

"What are you doing in my room?" he asked, confusion underlying his normally smooth voice.

"Rans?" I asked a bit groggily. "This is my room. Yours is across the hall."

He stared at me with a sort of *brain-rebooting-please-stand-by* expression on his face. That expression woke me up fast, and I slid off the bed to cross to him. That was when I noticed his extreme paleness. I mean… Rans was a vampire, yeah — and an English one, at that. He wasn't going to be winning any awards for 'Best Tan Lines' anytime soon. But this was the same sort of pale he'd been when I found him shot in my back yard.

It was the sort of paleness that belonged to a corpse, not a man.

"You don't look so good," I whispered in the understatement of the week. "What happened, what's wrong?"

Without even thinking about it, I took him by the arm and pulled him inside, closing the door behind us for privacy. He shook his head as if trying to dislodge something rattling around in his brain.

"I…" he said. "I don't…"

His voice trailed off and he lifted a hand to his forehead.

"Okay, you're scaring me now," I said.

I herded him toward the bed and pushed at his shoulders until he sat on the edge of it, his thighs bracketing mine as I stood in front of him. He glanced up at me through dark eyelashes from the slight disadvantage of height. Something about the look of vulnerability hiding just beneath the surface combined with the odd intimacy of our position to make me wonder if I should be backing off. Giving him space.

But—well, he'd saved me from a bunch of faeries and I'd had his dick in my mouth only yesterday, so maybe a bit of intimacy wasn't unreasonable at this point.

"Rans. Talk to me, please. Did something happen with Nigellus?"

A deep furrow formed between his brows. "No, I…" he trailed off. "That wasn't…" He shook his head sharply again. "Sorry. I seem to have… a bit of a hole in my memory. A new one, I mean."

Misgivings flooded me, but I tried to focus on the practical. He was pale and disoriented. He was a vampire. Those two facts could be related, right?

"Do you need blood?" I asked slowly.

His absent blue gaze turned inward, like he was taking stock.

There was a long pause. "Maybe so. I don't… feel right."

Yeah, you think? Sherlock Holmes would be proud right now.

He moved restlessly under my hands. "I should… find Edward."

"What?" I yelped, pushing him back down when he tried to rise. "No way. You are *not* drinking blood from an octogenarian butler!"

His eyes cleared a bit as he focused on me in consternation. "But—"

"No," I reiterated. "In fact, that's a great big *fuck, no.*" I drew in a breath to figure out an alternative, and the words tumbled out before I had a chance to run them through my brain-mouth filter. "Drink from me instead."

Oh, shit. Did I really just say that out loud?

Flashes of conversation flitted through my mind.

Your blood. It's unusually... what's the word I'm looking for? Stimulating.

Oh, dear. For an undead erection lasting more than four hours..."

Shit. This was a self-serving and totally uncool thing for me to be doing, wasn't it? Blue eyes sharpened.

"You're already weakening," he said. "That would only make it worse."

I shrugged carelessly. "No it won't. You feed from me first, and I'll, uh... I'll feed from you afterward."

The strange, shaky need I recognized from the night in Guthrie's penthouse was rising inside me. The heady desire to take, pull, consume... to draw pleasure from Rans' body into mine.

He was still staring at me intently. I couldn't tell if he was wavering or not.

"Maybe I still don't believe you about being part demon," I added, trying to tip the balance in my favor. "Maybe I want to see if having sex again really makes me stronger." I lifted one hand from his shoulder, cupping the elegant planes of his cheek. "You said it yourself. I'm weakening. Who else around here am I going to screw? Nigellus isn't really my type, and somehow I doubt Edward would be interested."

That did the trick. Evidently, Rans was hiding an unexpectedly territorial streak beneath that devil-may-care exterior. Maybe I was, too, because when I ended up on my back on the bed a moment later, my immediate response was *oh, hell yes.*

Glowing eyes blazed down at me, a hard-muscled body caging mine against the softness of the bed.

"What are you doing to me, Zorah Bright?" he asked.

"Feeding you, I hope," I said a bit breathlessly, "and then fucking you. Maybe between the two of us, we can manage to be a little less broken."

He let out a sharp huff of breath as though someone had hit him in the chest, and dropped his face to rest against the crook of my neck. Goose-flesh pebbled across my body at the feel of soft lips brushing my sensitive skin. I wanted to flip him over and rip his clothes off so I could get more of that feeling of skin-on-skin, but I suppose the suspense of waiting also had a certain piquancy to it.

A hand tangled in my curls, tipping my head back and exposing the column of my throat. Heat bloomed in my belly as Rans slid fangs into the delicate skin of my neck for the second time in our short acquaintance. And, yes, I knew my slutty reaction was still pretty fucked up, but this time I refused to feel guilty or weirded out about it.

The deep, drawing sensation seemed to have a direct line to my sex. My spine bowed as my body tried to arch off the bed… to get closer to the hard body poised above mine. I didn't lose consciousness this time—I guess whatever was ailing Rans right now hadn't left him as ravenous for blood as a gunshot to the chest, at least.

The razor sharp points of his fangs slipped free of my skin, and a tongue rasped over the twin wounds. *Vampire blood and saliva have healing properties*, I remembered distantly. Indeed, I couldn't feel any evidence of blood dripping from the wounds, and the burn of sensation that should have been pain — but wasn't, exactly — was already fading.

The pulse of need between my legs sure as hell wasn't fading, though. I bucked my hips up, seeking friction, and was rewarded with a rough growl of, "Bloody *hell*, woman." Fingers dragged one of the spaghetti straps of my silky nightgown over my shoulder until my right breast spilled out of its cup. Lips closed around the nub and I keened, trying to press more of the soft globe into that cool mouth.

It was so good… so good… but it wasn't what I really needed.

"Clothes," I gasped.

Rans made a low noise in his throat and his weight disappeared. The room was spinning, whether due to my blood loss or the fact that whatever blood I had left was currently pulsing and throbbing between my thighs, I wasn't sure. The vertigo was irritating, because it meant I couldn't fully appreciate the sight of Rans stripping out of the tailored trousers and button-down he'd worn for the flight from St. Louis.

I guess my blood had helped him, because he didn't seem to be unsteady anymore — though it was a bit hard to tell with the room moving in ponderous circles around me. I closed my eyes against the dizziness when hands slid the silken fabric of the nightgown up my thighs. My legs fell open of their own volition, making room for the cool body that settled between them.

When lips brushed my sex in a closed-mouth kiss, it drove a sharp, high-pitched noise from me. I arched, trying to get more, but the hands that had pushed my nightgown out of the way closed around my hips with a grip almost hard enough to bruise.

Rans seduced my sensitive folds with his lips the way another man might have seduced my mouth with a kiss. Teasing… questing lightly along the seam until my body bloomed under his touch, parting to invite him deeper.

I grasped handfuls of the green duvet, desperate for an anchor as I was dragged into the riptide and pulled under. The orgasm rolled over me as his clever tongue slid up my length to torture my clit with firm strokes. It left me reeling, still dizzy—unsure which direction was up and which was down.

And it *still* wasn't what I needed.

"More," I begged.

A moment later, he was stalking up the length of my body. One muscular arm hooked my left knee over his elbow, drawing my leg almost double against my body as he braced on his other hand and positioned himself over me.

"I suspect you're about to learn the meaning of the phrase, 'Be careful what you ask for,'" he said, and sheathed himself inside of me.

That was what I needed—the sweet nectar of his sexual energy a counterpoint to my body's pleasure as the heady stretch deepened into a delicious ache.

"Give it to me," I demanded. "Let me feel all of it…"

He let out a low, breathless noise and lowered his head, teasing the place he'd bitten earlier with lips and teeth as he began to move. I canted my hips to meet each slow thrust, the angle letting him drive deliciously deeper with every stroke.

This. *This* was heaven. I could feel his body giving itself to me, in counterpoint to the way mine had given itself to him when he'd drunk blood from me. We rocked together, his lips gradually working their way up my neck to tease the hinge of my jaw, brush at my ear, and then slide across my cheek in a series of butterfly kisses.

When his mouth slanted over mine, I shuddered in ecstasy at the intimacy of being connected in both places. *God…* I could taste myself on him. My lips parted, our tongues dueling as my body urged him ever closer to his own release. I could feel it coming. I wanted it. I *needed* it.

And then he was jerking free of the kiss, burying his head in the crook of my shoulder as his smooth strokes grew sloppy. His body jerked, the feeling of his pleasure flowing into me like a drug I'd never be able to get enough of. It flowed into my core, spreading to my limbs, making me strong. If I'd harbored any doubts as to what I was, that feeling erased them.

I was drawing sexual energy from his body as surely as he'd drawn blood from my veins.

Eventually he stilled, letting my leg slide free of his grip but not making any move to withdraw. He didn't let his weight sag onto me as I curled fingers through the dark hair at the nape of his neck, but I could feel his arm muscles trembling faintly on either side of me.

After a long moment, one of his arms snaked around my lower back, and somehow he rolled us over in a single smooth movement. I lay on top of him now, our flesh still joined.

"Thank you," I murmured into his smooth chest, draping myself over him like a blanket as I reveled in the feeling of completeness and wellbeing.

His hand traveled up and down the length of my spine in slow, firm strokes, and I could feel the rumble of his voice through my cheek as he spoke. "Thanking me already? I've just drunk succubus blood, pet. Even worse, my brain is still running in endless circles. Believe me when I say, you're not *nearly* done with me yet."

He rolled his hips as if to demonstrate, and my passage clamped around his cock—still hard and ready. As the sense of the words penetrated my happy cloud of contentedness, I moaned and pushed upright, bracing my hands on his broad shoulders. Fresh hunger rose inside me. When I lifted and lowered myself along his thick length, he looked up at me in challenge, one eyebrow lifting. His hands skimmed up my ribcage to cup my breasts, thumbs swiping across the tight points of my nipples.

I squeezed my inner muscles around him and rode him slowly, never breaking eye contact. "Sure you're not the one who should be careful what he asks for?" I quipped.

He thrust up, lifting my entire body. "Believe me, luv... I'm absolutely counting on it."

Nineteen

We didn't last the full four hours Nigellus had joked about, but it was definitely more than three hours later when we both lay curled together, sated in every sense of the word. I nestled against Rans' side, naked skin against naked skin, my head pillowed on his chest as I drew aimless patterns across his skin with my fingertips.

"Brain stopped working yet?" I murmured, scraping a fingernail over his nipple to make him shiver.

"Mm," he hummed in wordless agreement, burying his nose in my hair.

A nagging worry had taken up residence in the time since my libido had ceded control back to my intellect a few minutes ago. "Can you kick-start the old gray matter long enough to answer a question for me?" I asked, craning up to look at his face.

His eyes were closed and his expression, relaxed. "Depends on how complicated the question is."

I shrugged, disturbed that I hadn't been thinking about this before the fact rather than after. "It's just… should we have been using protection? I was on the pill until I had to go on the run three days ago. But…" I trailed off.

The hand that had been wrapped around my shoulder lifted to smooth my hair back. "It's fine," he said. "I couldn't do anything to you even if you were fully human—which you're not."

I relaxed a bit, but I also couldn't help remembering that my mother was supposed to have been infertile. That hadn't stopped her from having me.

"So…" I pressed, rolling up on an elbow so I could look down at him. "Is it an undead thing? Like, you can't father children because your sperm isn't viable?"

One eyelid peeled open, revealing a sliver of blue. "I'm a vampire," he deadpanned. "Don't you read books? I can't come inside unless I'm invited."

I blinked at him, torn between erupting into undignified laughter and hitting him in the face with a pillow. After a moment's debate, I opted for the pillow, and he batted it away half-heartedly.

"That is not remotely funny," I lied.

"Bollocks," he said. "That line is god-damned hilarious. But to answer your question seriously, I can't produce sperm and my body can't harbor microbes. I'm bloody *dead*, Zorah—if it could, I would've rotted back into the ground centuries ago."

I shuddered a bit. "Not an image I really needed… but thanks for the reassurance." I frowned at him. "You're a big fat liar, though. You waltzed right into my house without so much as a by-your-leave."

"It was a *joke*," he protested. "Ugh. Americans. No sense of humor whatsoever."

I boofed him again with the pillow for good measure before relenting and brushing a soft kiss against his lips. He smiled, his eyes slipping closed again.

"I'm going to clean up and go down to dinner," I said. "You should rest. You've slept way less than I have in the past couple of days. Do you need some more blood, though? I don't like this feeling that I've turned into some kind of sexual parasite on humanity."

His smile turned crooked and broken for a moment. "I'm not human anymore, luv. Haven't been for a very long time. And when it comes to being a parasite, believe me—no one beats a vampire."

"Even so—" I began.

He waved the words away. "I'm all right, Zorah. Might nap for a bit, though…"

It sounded like he was about two seconds from doing just that. I stroked a few strands of messy black hair away from his forehead. "You do that," I whispered.

Even after hearing his reassurance, I still wasn't sure how to feel about the fact that I'd clearly wiped him out with my succubus routine, while I, on the other hand, felt like freaking *superwoman*. I grabbed a quick shower in the en-suite and dressed, pulling my hair into a damp ponytail and not bothering with makeup. I wanted a word or three with our host, and looking pretty wasn't going to be a prerequisite for this conversation.

It was five minutes past seven when I entered the dining room, where Edward was arranging serving dishes in the center of the table. Nigellus sat at the head, with two other place settings arranged on either side of him.

"Good evening, my dear," he said. "Please, have a seat. Will Ransley be joining us this evening?"

I remained standing. "He's not feeling himself right now," I stated, watching Nigellus' face carefully for any reaction. "I left him napping."

The smooth, cool lines of our host's expression didn't so much as flicker. "That's unfortunate. Ah, well—I daresay he needs the rest. Our mutual friend does have a tendency to burn the candle at both ends."

Stepping forward, I let my hands rest on the high back of one of the waiting chairs. "What did you do to him earlier?" I asked.

A faint wash of surprise tipped Nigellus' eyebrows up. "Do to him?" he echoed. "Whatever do you mean?"

I didn't shift position or break eye contact. "It's a straightforward enough question. He was fine when you two left together, and when he came upstairs afterward he was a wreck. What did you do to him?"

Nigellus leaned back in his chair, his gaze boring into me. I had a feeling that on a normal day, I couldn't have stood up to that gaze for five seconds. Right now, though, I was pumped up on vampire sex mojo and I was damn well getting some answers.

"Ransley is like a son to me, Ms. Bright," Nigellus said slowly. "I assure you, I've done nothing to harm him."

I narrowed my eyes. "So he was fine when he left you after your little talk, and somewhere between your tête-à-tête and the upstairs bedroom, something happened to make a badass, seven-hundred-year-old sword-wielding vampire lose a chunk out of his memory and nearly stumble over his own feet trying to walk through a doorway? *Bullshit*."

Edward was watching me with a slightly wide-eyed expression. "I'll just go check on dessert, sir, shall I?" he asked, and beat a hasty retreat toward the kitchen.

"Answer me, damn it," I snapped.

Nigellus continued to regard me like I was a mildly interesting art exhibit, though I couldn't detect any hint of either anger or defensiveness in his demeanor.

"Ms. Bright," he began in that urbane voice, "you've only recently been thrust into this world, and there are many things you don't yet know about Ransley's past. This is completely understandable, of course, since there are many things *he* doesn't know about his past. Ransley is… somewhat obsessed with unraveling the mystery surrounding his escape from the fate that befell his fellow vampires."

"And what fate was that, exactly?" I interrupted. "You said they were killed in the war—every single one of them except him. How is that even possible?"

"They fell to a Fae weapon," he said. "One that utilized a form of magic never seen before."

My breath caught, but I refused to be side-tracked. "And Rans?"

"That is the mystery, is it not? One he seems determined to solve, no matter the cost." For the first time, Nigellus looked away, and I thought I could detect a hint of frustration in his manner. His voice was quieter when he continued. "Perhaps I should not support him in his self-appointed quest. Yet whenever I come across anything anomalous that seems as though it might be related, I share it with him."

"Was that what you wanted to talk to him about earlier?"

"Indeed it was. I think discussing the subject is sometimes... harder for him than he lets on. I assure you, though, that he did seem all right when he left me. Merely distracted."

I mulled that for a few moments. Nigellus seemed utterly sincere, and it wasn't the first indication I'd glimpsed that my vampiric knight in black leather was... not completely okay. If he was suffering from some kind of centuries-old PTSD, I supposed it could fit with memory lapses and the desire he'd expressed earlier to shut off his endlessly circling brain for a bit.

"Okay," I said eventually. "I can understand that. And I apologize for storming in here and spouting accusations at you."

"You're his friend, and you're worried about him," Nigellus said without rancor. "You may not believe it, but that pleases me. It really does.

Ransley has many friends, but none, I think, who might be inclined to protect him from his own worst impulses. His recklessness concerns me at times, as does his single-mindedness when it comes to the subject of the war."

"Well," I said, "that recklessness recently saved me from ending up a prisoner of some very nasty characters. But I don't want to see him hurt, Nigellus."

Nigellus smiled. "You've already proven that most effectively, my dear. Now, would you care to dine with me this evening? I fear the dishes are getting cold."

I shook my head, not feeling hungry and not wanting to prolong what was fast becoming an awkward conversation. "I think I'll pass, though I truly do appreciate your hospitality."

He shrugged easily. "You're demonkin, Zorah. There aren't so many demons that we can afford to turn our backs on our own."

I tried on a smile, though it felt a bit forced. "I do have one request," I said. "I don't suppose you know a way that I could contact my father in Chicago without putting either of us in danger? I have his cell phone and landline numbers, as well as his email."

Nigellus looked thoughtful. "Perhaps. Why don't you speak to Edward about it? He's the expert on such things. Personally, I have a hard time keeping up with human technology these days. Everything changes so quickly."

"All right," I said, trying to hide my skepticism. Normally when I was looking for tech advice, asking the eighty-year-old butler wasn't my first instinct, but… "I'll, uh, see if he has a moment before he serves dessert."

———◆———

Forty-five minutes later, I ascended the stairs in something of a daze. Edward's rheumy eyes had lit up with excitement the moment I'd asked about contacting Dad securely, and I now knew more than I'd ever wanted to about using voice over IP across a secure VPN based in the Netherlands.

After hearing me relate the concerns Rans had raised about bringing Fae attention to my father, Edward had insisted that he be the one to actually place the call. We devised a sort of informal code that would make it sound like a routine call relating to a shipping screw-up, but which would—hopefully, anyway—make it clear to my father that I was safe, but couldn't make it to Chicago.

That had been the plan, at least.

Too bad it hadn't worked out that way. Now, my heart was pounding with fear, remembering the speed and thoroughness with which Caspian had managed to dismantle my entire life. I stumbled into the guest room, my eyes falling on Rans' naked form in the bed—the duvet thrown carelessly across the lower half of his body.

He blinked awake immediately at the sound of the door opening, looking much less out-of-it than he had earlier.

"I need to leave," I blurted, standing frozen two steps from the doorway.

He frowned. "Pressing engagement elsewhere, luv?" he asked in a voice made gravelly by sleep. "The sex wasn't *that* bad, was it?"

But I only shook my head impatiently. "I have to get to Chicago," I insisted, forging ahead. "My dad's in trouble."

Rans hefted himself into a sitting position, still frowning—the duvet slipping dangerously. "Tell me you didn't call him."

"No. Edward did, through a secure VPN… thing," I said quickly. "He was going to pretend to be a customer service representative so no one would suspect anything, but…" I cut myself off, swallowing hard.

"But?" Rans prompted.

"Dad's cell phone is out of service and his landline has been disconnected," I said in a rush. "He's lived in that condo for more than eight years! He didn't have any plans to leave. And he's an *accountant.* No way did he forget to pay the bills or something."

"Damn. That's… not good," Rans agreed grimly.

I scrubbed a hand over my face. It was shaking.

"I need to get up there," I said. "If you could… I dunno… help me get through security again and get onto a plane, I can probably handle things on the other end. I've got Guthrie's ID still, and—"

"No," Rans said evenly, cutting off my disjointed babble. "You're not running straight into a Fae trap on my watch."

"*I have to help him.*"

"Of course you do, Zorah. He's your father," Rans said, bringing the sting of unwanted tears to my eyes. "But you can do it the smart way, or you can charge in like they expect you to and cock up the whole thing. That won't help anyone, will it?"

I took several deep breaths. "Then what do you suggest? I can't just leave him in their hands while I dick around in Atlantic City waiting for a better plan to present itself."

He regarded me thoughtfully for a long moment before he spoke. "I don't think this has occurred to you yet, but there's another possibility here."

My brow furrowed. "What do you mean?"

Rans sighed. "Look. Someone tipped off Caspian that you were going to take a bus out of St. Louis. From the way you described it, there were only two people who knew about your plans."

The bottom dropped out of my stomach. "No," I said immediately, shaking my head.

"You need to at least keep it in mind," Rans insisted. "Otherwise you're setting yourself up to be played."

"*No*," I repeated more forcefully, even though the seeds of doubt had been irreparably planted as soon as he'd said the words. "I don't believe it."

"You don't have to believe it. You just have to be aware that it's a possibility." He ran a hand through his hair. "Now. If you charge in without a thought in your head for strategy, you're going to ensure that I took a silver knife to the shoulder for nothing. Let me talk to someone I know in Chicago and see what I can learn. When we have a better idea of the landscape, we'll go there together."

I swallowed, trying to moisten my dry throat. "Why?" I asked. "Why are you still going out of your way for me?"

The half-smile he gave me was a bit wistful. "Told you earlier, luv. You're my loose thread. I pulled you, and now your dad seems to have popped free. I haven't unraveled the jumper yet, though. Still plenty of stitches left."

I chewed my lower lip. "All right. Just... don't take too long."

He slid out of bed, all graceful lines, and crossed to stand in front of me, unconcerned by his nakedness. I gazed up at clear blue eyes set in a serious face. His hand cupped my cheek, mirroring the gesture I'd extended to him earlier. Again, I felt the sting of tears, and I blinked them back ruthlessly.

"I won't," he promised. "Trust me, Zorah."

My eyes slipped closed, and I nodded in reluctant agreement.

Twenty

Two days later, I white-knuckled my way through the touchdown at O'Hare airport in Chicago. This time, I'd been less surprised when Rans tangled my fingers with his for both the take-off and landing. We'd also flown through a thunderstorm en route. Winds buffeting the delicate structure of the aircraft until I thought I'd bite straight through my lower lip, but Rans' claim of being statistically crash-proof had thankfully held.

"We'll be meeting my contact here at the airport," he said as we disembarked. "He's been looking into things, so once we speak to him, we can decide what to do and go from there."

We'd only brought a single carryon bag each, so we didn't have to wait at the baggage claim like we had in Philly.

"Why didn't you pack the pointy things this time?" I asked. "I mean, why take the trouble to get them to Atlantic City, but not here?"

"Nigellus doesn't keep weapons," Rans told me. "My contact here does, should we have need of any."

Somehow, that seemed ominous, though I couldn't quite put my finger on why. It was probably a moot point in my case, regardless—it's not like I was going to be taking out anyone with a sword. Indeed, I'd been freaked out enough by the silver knife Rans had gifted me, that I'd taken advantage of the delay in Atlantic City to have Edward get the best price for it he could at an area pawn shop.

I had no idea how to use a dagger, but I was pretty sure I could come up with a use for an extra couple of hundred bucks at some point.

Rans' mysterious contact had told him yesterday that there was something going on among the Fae in Chicago. Whatever the details, it was being kept secret at high levels. My gut was convinced it had to do with Dad, and Rans had agreed it seemed likely.

We exited the airport from Terminal 2, heading for the arrivals and departures area. Rans scanned the line of cars as we walked. My gaze followed his, and my feet stumbled to a halt so abruptly that the lady behind me nearly ran into my back. A black Mercedes sat next to the curb, sleek and threatening.

Rans noticed my stumble and looked back, pausing to wait for me as I unglued my feet from the pavement. "Not who you're thinking of, luv. Sorry—I should have warned you. That'll be our ride."

"*That's* your contact?" I asked warily.

He made an affirmative noise and continued toward the Merc. "Yes. He's Fae, but try not to hold it against him."

Tension gathered in my shoulders. I tried to rationalize it—who better to find out what the damned faeries were up to than one of their own number? And if I started pre-judging people based on what species they belonged to, what would that make me? No group was made up of all good people or all bad people. That kind of thinking was how wars and other horrific things got started.

A graceful figure emerged from the driver's side of the car. His golden hair hung loose, the long strands teased by the wind coming off Lake Michigan. His face boasted the same preternaturally attractive features as the other Fae I'd seen, but at least his taste in suits was better. Rather than wearing a stupid, ugly tie, he'd unbuttoned the top couple of buttons on his dress shirt. Black ink was visible on the exposed triangle of skin, tattoos winding up to the base of his neck like questing tree roots in reverse.

I felt the same unpleasant crawling sensation that I'd felt in the presence of Caspian Werther and his two guards, even though this Fae didn't give me more than a cursory glance. With luck, that meant that he wasn't the same kind of skeevy creeper the others had been. A girl could hope, anyway.

As he circled the car's hood to approach us, Rans tensed. An instant later, I saw a half-dozen police officers exiting from unmarked vehicles parked behind the Merc.

"You two are in my custody," said the Fae, gesturing the police to surround us. "Don't resist, or things will take a decidedly unfortunate turn for both of you."

My heart thundered in sudden panic, and I looked wildly toward Rans. He was unarmed, and even though he *had* managed to overcome three men in the parking lot behind the bus station in St. Louis, there were more than twice that number here.

The police were all conspicuously armed with handguns. True, a shotgun blast had failed to kill Rans, but it had sure as hell put him down for the count before he recovered. And a gunshot would put me in the ground as surely as one had put my mother there, some twenty years ago.

Rans stared hard at the Fae. For an interminable moment, I felt him poised to act—but... act *how*? Would I be expected to fight? To run? To drop to the ground and try to stay the hell out of his way?

The Fae merely returned Rans' fiery blue gaze, no hint of expression on his beautiful face. I stood frozen, trembling, unsure of what was coming next. And then, Rans subsided, silently leashing that barely restrained promise of violence under a stony facade of calm.

"It's all right, luv," he told me. "Don't resist them."

"*All right*?" I asked in disbelief, looking at the circle of cops around us. How in the hell was this *all right*?

"Making a scene right now wouldn't be good," he said in a low voice.

His blue eyes flashed at me, and I felt a brush of something against my mind like a breath of calm. I shook my head, fighting it off.

"Don't you *ever* try to do that to me," I growled.

He continued to stare, but the sense of someone else trying to influence my mind slipped away. The cops moved forward, dragging Rans' arms behind his back and cuffing his wrists.

"Trust me, *JoAnne*," he said, emphasizing the fake name that he and Guthrie had acquired for me. "This is not the time or place to attract attention."

"Enough chatter," said the Fae asshole. "Get them in the car."

A policeman cuffed my wrists as well, and I had to fight not to succumb to the same panic that those words had engendered the last time I'd heard them. *You're not alone this time. You're not alone... you're not alone...*

I repeated the words like a mantra, feeling my heart thud against my ribs.

"Wait," said our captor, and gestured to Rans with his chin. "Hold that one still for a moment."

Rans narrowed his eyes as the Fae lifted one hand, his fingers moving through the air as though reaching for something invisible.

"*Seriously*?" Rans asked, his expression looking like he'd tasted something sour.

The Fae only raised a sharp eyebrow. A diaphanous halo of light surrounded his hand, and for a moment, the slide of shadows made it look as though the tattoos at his throat were moving. Shifting restlessly across his skin. I looked around us, thinking other people must surely be able to see what was happening.

The passersby around us walked past without giving us a second glance—as though seeing uniformed cops handcuffing people while Legolas from Lord of the fucking Rings stood there with his hand glowing was a regular occurrence for them. I gritted my teeth to keep from calling out for help. It hadn't worked in St. Louis, and probably wouldn't work any better now.

Rans was still glaring as Legolas murmured a rapid-fire series of words I couldn't understand. He flicked his long fingers, and the glow surrounding his hand like fireflies streamed toward Rans and wound around his body. The glimmering lights spiraled around him before appearing to sink into his body and disappearing.

"Rans?" I asked—terrified, and with no freaking clue what was happening. I realized after the name left my mouth that I should have said *John*, the way he'd said *JoAnne*. I really, *really* sucked at this fugitive shit.

"It's just a warding spell," Rans said through gritted teeth.

If I hadn't been fighting panic, I might've had a couple of spare brain cells to devote to the idea of magic apparently being real. Goddamnit, I was already running *this* close to capacity after the past few days. I was not fucking prepared to deal with glowy hands and faerie spells.

Legolas gestured toward the cops, indicating that they should resume putting us in the back of the black Mercedes. I flopped ungracefully onto the upholstery, trying with little success to find a way to sit comfortably with my hands cuffed behind me. Rans followed a moment later with considerably more stoicism and less clumsiness. The door slammed shut, locks clicking with an air of chilling finality. The trunk closed, which I guessed meant the cops had thrown our luggage into the car.

I noticed there were no controls for either locks or windows on the inside of our doors.

Of course, Legolas had controls on *his* door. The driver's window rolled down, and he ordered the cops to leave. I craned around, watching them pile back into their unmarked cars and pull away. When they were gone, Rans met our captor's eyes in the rearview mirror.

"Oy, I'm being pretty fucking patient here, Tinkerbell," he said. "I've gotta say, though—my patience is in fairly short supply these days."

"Quiet," Legolas told him flatly, "or I'll shut you up myself."

His unnaturally green eyes grew intense, and he murmured more words in that unfamiliar language before a new glow surrounded both Rans and me in the back seat. I gasped in shock as Rans' appearance melted into something utterly different—ash blonde hair, face younger and far less striking, and carrying a bit of softness around the waist. Even his distinctive blue eyes were now an unremarkable shade of earthy brown.

Something made me look down at myself. My bare upper arms were pale now, rather than dusky, and I had thick curves that were completely different from my usual slender frame. Bewildered, my eyes flew back to the plain features that had, a moment ago, belonged to a dark angel sculpted by Raphael. Rans shook his head at me, a quelling gesture.

I bit my lip, sitting tense and silent as the car's engine purred, pulling us out into traffic and toward the highway. Legolas drove us in a generally westerly direction, based on the glimpses I got of the sun peeking through the clouds. The clock on the car's dashboard was flashing, not with the familiar *twelve – twelve – twelve*, but rather with a jumble of random illuminated segments that looked like gibberish. As best I could tell, it was about an hour later when he pulled into a long private driveway.

The bustle of the city had given way to something midway between suburban and rural surroundings. The house that was revealed as we negotiated a turn in the tree-lined drive was only a few paint chips and broken windows away from being the next hot property for filming a horror movie. With two stories and a generous attic, it must have been an impressive residence when it was new. The grounds were obviously huge; the driveway itself must have been nearly a quarter mile long.

Legolas parked in a spacious circle drive, and two figures emerged from the front door of the house. He got out of the car to meet them. After a brief discussion, the two newcomers—also Fae, I was sure—opened our doors and pulled us out of the back seat.

"Take them to the basement," Legolas ordered, lending new urgency to my growing panic.

This was turning into everything I'd feared in St. Louis. If we entered that basement, would we ever see the sky again? Rans was still wearing his *sucked-on-a-lemon* expression, for all that the face it adorned was unfamiliar. For the thousandth time in the last hour, I wondered how far my growing trust toward him could reasonably be expected to reach.

I tensed, ready to plant my feet and struggle, but his brows drew together in warning. *Don't*, he mouthed, pinning me with a hard, mud-brown gaze.

The only thing that held me back was my memory of just how pointless my panicked struggles against Caspian's guards had been. Even if I could get free, the road was almost a quarter mile away, and it had been dead quiet when we approached this place. Where did I think I was going to go?

I had a phone, but no one to call. I was in an unfamiliar city, and the one person I knew here was the one who was missing—my dad. Lack of any kind of usable plan meant that in the end, I let the Fae guard holding my arm propel me into the house and down a functional, poorly lit stairway to an unfinished basement.

The place had been converted into cells, and that *was* enough to make me balk. By that time, though, it was too late. My captor hefted me painfully by the upper arms and manhandled me— *fairy-handled me?*—into the largest cell. Rans and his captor were right behind me, followed by Legolas.

His cool green gaze played over the two guards. "Leave us. The prisoners are to have no food or water for twenty-four hours. I will tolerate no interruptions during the initial interrogation period… disregard my orders at your peril."

The lackeys dipped their heads in what almost looked like bows. "Yes, Liege," said the one on the right, and both of them trooped out hastily, closing the door as they went.

I swallowed hard, knowing I was breathing too fast and in danger of hyperventilating. Clammy sweat had broken out across my body as the door slammed shut, leaving me trapped with a creature that made every nerve in my body tingle with my need to be elsewhere.

I knew that succumbing to a panic attack right now was the worst conceivable thing I could do, but when had I ever been able to stop one when it started to happen? I tried to focus on Rans… to use him as a way to calm myself. But Rans didn't look like Rans anymore. The face of the person standing next to me against the cold cell wall was a stranger's.

Legolas turned his attention on me, his head tilting in interest as he examined me. "Now, what in Mab's green garden do we have here?" he asked, looking at me like I was a puzzle he intended to disassemble into its constituent parts.

He took a step forward. Panic swallowed me. It was a different feeling than any of the other dozens and dozens of times my mind had betrayed me in such a way over the years. Instead of my vision tunneling in and my chest aching, the unbearable pressure exploded outward, as though my body had become the epicenter of a shockwave.

"*Zorah*!" Rans shouted.

Twenty-One

The invisible wave hit Legolas, who staggered back a single step before straightening. His green eyes dilated until the black of his pupils threatened to swallow his irises, a look of unrestrained hunger twisting his too-handsome face. A fresh wash of fear slid over me, but a moment later, I felt the true results of my panic-fueled handiwork.

Sexual energy began to flow out of the Fae's body, and into mine. I bared my teeth, feeling my own hunger rise.

"Zorah, *stop*," Rans said in a low tone.

But I didn't want to stop. I wanted to drain this creature in front of me until he was nothing but an empty husk. I wanted to see this Fae on his knees, begging me to stop… or begging me *not* to stop. I wanted—

The connection between us snapped with a sharp burst of agony on my end, cutting off the flow of raw power. Fury hardened the Fae's features into cold marble, and he closed the distance between us, lifting a hand toward my throat.

It was glowing.

Movement caught my peripheral vision. An instant later, white vapor swirled in front of me, solidifying into a human form in the space between one ragged breath and the next. Rans knocked the Fae's hand away, sparks flying between them like an electrical line shorting out.

"Fucking… *enough*, already. *Both of you*," Rans growled. "Jesus Christ, Alby. I don't exactly have the patience of a saint today."

My mouth worked, no words coming out at first.

"*What*. The *hell*. Is going on?" I managed, my voice an unpleasant, raucous squeak.

"*What is she*?" Legolas hissed.

"Trouble, mostly," Rans said in a flat tone. "Specifically, trouble that you don't lay a fucking hand on, unless you want to lose that hand."

He and the Fae were squared off, while I was still more-or-less cowering behind Rans' back. I shoved my way out from behind him, noticing distantly that he was now once again his normal self, rather than a plain-faced, slightly pudgy blonde guy.

"I'm assuming," Rans began, "that because you weakened the warding spell you used to bind me, it means I don't actually need to start ripping your wings off, Tinkerbell. But it would be good if you started talking. This cell reeks of security and silencing charms, so I assume it's safe to have a proper chat now.

"Answer the question, bloodsucker," Legolas snarled. "What is she?"

"*She* is standing right here!" I pointed out, and received a narrow green glare in response.

"Zorah is the offspring of a human and a cambion," Rans said.

"Impossible," the Fae spat.

"That's what *I* said," Rans agreed. "But you felt it, just now."

I cleared my throat, about done with being talked about in the third person. "Which brings us back to the very relevant question—*what the hell just happened*?"

The Fae frowned at me. "You don't know?"

"*Would I be asking you if I did*?" I exploded.

"You panicked and started sucking energy from our host," Rans said patiently. "Which, of course, you should *in no way* be able to do. Especially against someone with magic as powerful as his."

I mulled that over, seeing how the idea fit with what I'd just experienced. It fit… pretty well, actually. Legolas was still scowling at me, the look not sitting well on his pretty-boy features.

Great. So, magic was real, the guy I'd slept with twice now could disappear and reappear at will, and apparently I could suck sex energy out of horny faeries if I was freaked out enough. This week really couldn't get any better.

"I'd apologize," I began slowly, "if I weren't currently handcuffed in an interrogation cell in your basement."

"Hand over the key, mate—for fuck's sake," Rans ordered, holding a hand out palm up. "Then maybe we can start over from the beginning."

After a long look, the Fae pulled a key out of his pocket and passed it over. I blinked, trying to rearrange things in my still panic-fuzzed mind to accommodate this new twist. Rans eased me around and a moment later, the handcuffs clicked open. I rubbed my wrists, my eyes caught anew by my pale skin and short fingers.

I looked up at the Fae mistrustfully.

Rans sighed. "Zorah Elaine Bright, this is Albigard of the Unseelie Court. Alby, Zorah. And may I just add that both of you are currently serious pains in my lily-white arse."

Albigard and I remained silent, still watching each other warily.

"Give me strength," Rans muttered, barely audible.

"Am I to understand," Albigard began, "That this demonkin has no control over her powers?"

"I'm still standing right here, *Tinkerbell*!" I snapped.

His face darkened, but he smoothed the expression an instant later. "My apologies, demonkin. You don't have control of your powers?"

I swallowed, just now realizing that by pressing the point, it meant I'd have to deal with this Fae directly. I thought I caught a twitch of Rans' lips, and silently vowed bitter retribution on him if he was in any way amused by this situation.

"I didn't realize I *had* any 'powers' until just now," I said cautiously.

Green eyes held mine for a long beat before Albigard gave a small nod, as if to himself. "Then I extend forgiveness for your violation of my person. Endeavor not to repeat it, or I may grow to be less forgiving."

A smart-ass remark was on the tip of my tongue, but I swallowed it back upon realizing that

I'd apparently just sexually assaulted a faerie so I could feed from him. "I honestly didn't intend to do it," I said instead. "Now, if we could just address the part where we're still locked in a cell in your creepy dungeon-basement, everything'll be peachy."

I felt jittery... almost itchy, like I'd taken a hit of bad drugs. If this was my brain on faerie *animus*, I was never straying from vampire juice again. My eyes flicked sideways to Rans, and I looked away quickly.

"Seriously, Alby," Rans was saying, "there'd better be a good excuse for this farce. When I suggested meeting at the airport, I didn't expect us to be joined by a full squad of Chicago's boys in blue."

Albigard exhaled sharply and took a step away, running a hand through his fine, straight hair. The movement drained some of the tension from the atmosphere, as well.

"Something big is going on in this city," the Fae said. "Big, and secretive."

He waved a careless hand at me, and tingles rushed along my skin. When I looked down, my appearance had returned to normal.

"And whatever this big, secretive thing is, it's tied up with the human man I told you about?" Rans pressed.

"Apparently," Albigard said, sounding suddenly tired. "Of course, once the higher-ups realize you're tied up in it somehow, they'll be after you in force—assuming they aren't after you already. You'll be safe here for a bit, but I had to glamour you to make you seem like random prisoners. The human law enforcement officers I used at the airport don't know enough to be a problem, but only one of the two guards here is trustworthy."

Rans nodded. "I figured it was something like that. Though a bit of warning wouldn't have gone amiss, you know."

Albigard waved the words away as though they were a mere annoyance. "There may well have been listening charms attached to the automobile. You're here; no one is aware of your presence for the moment. I fail to see the issue."

"And my father?" I asked, ready to move past the bullshit even if Albigard's proximity *did* still make me want to crawl out of my skin.

The Fae's lips pressed into a thin, bloodless line. "I will take you both to the residence that Darryl Bright is listed as owning, though we should not linger there."

"Wait," I said. "How are we going to sneak past your guards and get out of the house? I thought you didn't want anyone knowing we were here."

Albigard gave me a look that implied I was mentally deficient. "I will transport you there magically, of course. Though I suppose I should still refresh your glamours, first."

I stared at him. "I have no idea what that means. But if it gets me to Dad's condo, then let's stop standing around and fucking *do it*."

"You heard the lady," Rans said, in the tone of someone who was about ready to be done with the day's bullshit. I could sympathize.

Albigard summoned his glowy magic again, and moments later Rans and I were once again disguised. Presumably, this was the glamour he'd mentioned. I twisted my newly pale hand back and forth, fascinated.

My attention was wrenched away when the Fae described a large oval shape with a smooth movement of his hand. A blazing gateway formed in thin air, tall and wide enough for a person to slip through.

I gaped at the hole in reality. "Oh, my god. You can make *portals*? I had a friend in high school who freaking *loved* that game."

"Come," Albigard said, ignoring my words even though irritation practically rolled off of him in waves.

I couldn't help casting a glance at Rans, trying to telegraph 'Is this safe?' without actually having to say it aloud. I had a sneaking suspicion that doing anything else to piss off the portalmaster right now would be ill advised.

"It's fine, luv," Rans said, taking my oddly unfamiliar hand in his.

He led me into the gap in the air. I squeezed my eyes shut as I stepped through, a wave of disorientation passing over me. When I opened my eyes, I was… someplace else. Someplace that should have been familiar, except that a tornado had torn through the familiarity.

Albigard stepped through after us, and the portal shrank to a point before disappearing completely. I looked around the room, a sinking feeling taking root in my stomach.

"Is this the place?" Rans asked.

"Yes," I whispered, not wanting it to be true.

My father's home had been torn apart—furnishings upended and broken, personal belongings shattered and torn to pieces. It wasn't immediately obvious to my untrained eye whether the wholesale destruction was the result of a struggle, or whether it was the result of a thorough—and callous—search for something hidden.

Either way, it was clear from the unnatural stillness of the place that my father wasn't here.

In eight years, I'd only been here five times… maybe six. Each visit had been tense and uncomfortable, punctuated by low-pitched arguments and hurtful comments. I walked forward in a daze, my eyes trying to reassemble the broken objects around me into a picture of normalcy. My gaze caught on a corner of colorful cloth, faded from its original vibrancy by the passage of time. I leaned down to grab it, tugging it out from behind the overturned table where it had been largely hidden.

Shaking, I clutched the torn quilt—a crazy patchwork of pink, blue, and lavender that had always decorated my parents' bed when I was a child. My knees went wobbly, and I sank to the ground.

My dad was the only family I had left. And now he was gone. Was this destruction my fault? It seemed likely. Why on earth had I ever thought it would be a good idea to call him for help?

Family members make excellent leverage, Rans had said. And, hey, what do you know? It turned out he was right.

"I'm going after him," I said, looking up at the vampire from my pathetic hunched position on the floor. "With or without you, I'm going to find him and get him back."

Rans drew breath to speak, but Albigard beat him to it.

"Until I can figure out a way to better disguise your presence in the city, you're not going anywhere except back to the basement cell," the Fae stated, clearly unimpressed by my incipient emotional breakdown.

"The fuck I am," I snarled at him, my anger swirling dangerously.

Rans stepped between us, cutting off my view of Albigard. He crouched in front of me, sitting on his heels, covering my hands with his where they twisted in the fabric of the old quilt.

He was wearing a calm, rational expression that only pissed me off more. I figured I wasn't going to like what he said next, and—*surprise, surprise*—I was right.

"We have no way of knowing the circumstances of your father's disappearance, Zorah, and the moment you start poking around and asking the wrong kinds of questions to the wrong kinds of people, the Fae will know you're here." His low voice was not without empathy, but I didn't care.

I jerked my hands away, not letting go of the quilt. "The Fae already know I'm here!" I snapped, glaring at Albigard.

"*One* Fae knows you're here," Rans corrected, his tone hardening. "And he's the one who put himself at risk to bring us to this flat so we could investigate. Now, are you going to do something suicidal in pursuit of your internal script that says you can only rely on yourself? Or are you going to accept help when it's fucking offered to you?"

I stared at the vampire who'd done nothing but try to keep me safe, and beyond him, to the Fae who made my skin crawl. I let my gaze wander around the destroyed condo, the fear that my father had been taken against his will warring with the fear that he *hadn't* been taken against his will.

Rans' observation that only my dad and I had known I was getting a bus ticket in St. Louis pricked at me like a thorn embedded in skin. But either way, I needed answers and I was damned well going to get them.

"My only goal is to find my father," I said, meeting Rans' gaze again. "From this moment, that's the one thing I care about. As long as it's your goal, too, we're good. If I get a hint that it's not, then we have a serious problem."

"Agreed," Rans said after the barest hesitation, "on the condition that you listen when someone tells you you're about to do something foolish."

I turned my burning gaze to Albigard, who gave me a look that said he didn't consider any 'problem' I might pose to be a serious one. When I continued to glare at him, he looked like he wanted to roll his eyes. I didn't back down from that look, crawling skin or no, and eventually he gave me a careless nod of agreement.

"Good," I said, my eyes falling on a broken picture frame on the floor near me. My mother and father gazed out at me from behind shards of shattered glass, smiling and happy. "So... where do we start?"

End of Book One

Zorah's story continues in *The Last Vampire: Book Two.*

To discover more books by this author, visit www.rasteffan.com

Printed in Great Britain
by Amazon

37283064R00131